Jake seemed to fill her small room

Claire watched him with a growing sense of unease as he strolled around, very much at home, inspecting the books, the framed Picasso prints.

On an impulse she said, "By the way, what happened to the blonde?"

Now that got a reaction from him. He turned around slowly and gave her a long, suspicious look. "What blonde?"

"Oh, come on. I was there. I saw the whole thing. None of my business, of course," she added. "I was just curious."

To her astonishment, he turned an interesting shade of red. "That was just a bet," he said in an offhand tone.

"I see. Something like a dare."

"You could put it like that."

"Do you always feel compelled to accept every challenge you're given?" she asked lightly.

Rosemary Hammond lives on the West Coast but has traveled extensively with her husband throughout the United States, Mexico and Canada. She loves to write and has been fascinated by the mechanics of fiction ever since her college days. She reads extensively, enjoying everything from Victorian novels to mysteries, spy stories and, of course, romances.

Books by Rosemary Hammond

HARLEQUIN ROMANCE

2601—FULL CIRCLE
2655—TWO DOZEN RED ROSES
2674—THE SCENT OF HIBISCUS
2817—PLAIN JANE
2968—MODEL FOR LOVE

HARLEQUIN PRESENTS

802—THE HABIT OF LOVING
859—MALIBU MUSIC
896—LOSER TAKE ALL
985—ALL MY TOMORROWS
1017—CASTLES IN THE AIR
1136—ONE STOLEN MOMENT

Game Plan

Rosemary Hammond

Harlequin Books

TORONTO • NEW YORK • LONDON
AMSTERDAM • PARIS • SYDNEY • HAMBURG
STOCKHOLM • ATHENS • TOKYO • MILAN

Original hardcover edition published in 1989
by Mills & Boon Limited

ISBN 0-373-03026-6

Harlequin Romance first edition January 1990

Printed in U.S.A.

CHAPTER ONE

WHILE she waited for her two o'clock appointment to arrive, Claire stood at the window of her tiny office looking out at the rolling lawns and winding paths of the small college campus. It was a lovely autumn day, warm for October, with towering maples dotting the scene with brilliant splashes of bright red and gold.

Underneath the trees, clusters of students lounged on the grass, studying and chatting, while others walked or wheeled their bicycles along the paths. There were even one or two on roller-skates, and, she saw with a slight twinge of envy, several couples lying on the lawn locked in passionate embrace.

Claire turned away from the window and glanced at her watch. It was past two o'clock, and her first appointment of the afternoon, a strapping young football player who had just flunked his senior English mid-term exams, was already ten minutes late. She knew exactly how it would go.

There was at least one of them every term. He would turn on the little-boy charm, give her a pathetic story about not being able to continue on the football team if he didn't pass the course, and plead with her to give him a better grade on the test than they both knew he deserved.

There was a rap on the door, and she looked up to

see her gigantic athlete lumber inside, filling the small space with his enormous bulk and height. He grinned sheepishly at her.

'Sorry I'm late, Miss Talbot. We were discussing *Beowulf*, and I just couldn't tear myself away.'

Claire gave him a cool, assessing gaze. She recognised all the signs: the same old combination of respectful humility and arrogant impertinence. He'd have to learn that she was not as easily manipulated as the adoring schoolgirls who clustered around him and his team-mates as though they were Greek gods just descended from Mount Olympus.

She put on her most severe expression. 'Sit down, Scott. I'll be very interested to hear your thoughts on *Beowulf* before I make up my mind about your grade.'

The blond giant's face fell. He gave her one stricken, open-mouthed look and stumbled to the chair beside her desk.

When it was over, and a chastened Scott had withdrawn to nurse his wounds, Claire steeled herself for the next appointment, a track star this time. It would only be more of the same. With a resigned sigh she pulled towards her the tall stack of blue books. She might as well work on the rest of the mid-term papers Curtis had given her to grade while she waited.

When she finally emerged, it was four o'clock and there was no sign of the track star. She might as well pack up and go home. His test score was even worse than Scott's, and she could live without another messy confrontation that day.

She was just stuffing the last of the blue books into

her briefcase when the door flew open and a very tall, very angry-looking man burst inside. He stood on the threshold for a second, his lean face set and grim, his narrowed eyes raking the room, as though he was looking for something to attack.

He took one look at her and came charging over to her desk, then stood there, glaring down at her, his hands stuffed in his trouser pockets, his thin mouth clamped into a firm line. He was so tall that she had to crane her neck to meet his challenging gaze, a rare experience for a woman who stood five feet nine in her stockinged feet.

She drew herself up to her full height and stared back at him. 'Yes?' she said frostily. 'May I help you?'

'What's this I hear about you flunking Scott Cunningham?' he demanded loudly.

Claire bridled at his tone, which was more—much more—than merely challenging. It was downright hostile. 'I beg your pardon,' she said stiffly. 'And who might you be?'

'Is it true?' he barked, brushing aside the question.

'May I ask what business that is of yours?' she enquired loftily.

'Listen, lady,' he bit out, 'will you just answer my question? Did you or did you not give Scott a failing grade in his senior English mid-term?'

She lifted her chin and met his eyes directly. They were an arresting shade of green, with a flashing glint in them that reminded her of a broken shard of glass. He was a slightly rumpled-looking man, with a thick shock of dark chestnut-coloured hair and an athlete's build.

Then she recognised him. It was Jake Donovan, Rainier College's football coach, and she had to admit that the fate of his star players probably was his business, after all. He was wearing a tweed sports jacket, his striped tie was loosened, the top button of his white shirt undone, and she found his whole demeanour distinctly menacing.

'Yes,' she said finally. 'I did.'

'Aha!' he said, nodding with satisfaction, as though he had just caught her in the act of a terrible crime.

Claire was having none of that. 'And I might add,' she announced in a clear voice, 'that it was a grade he richly deserved.'

'Well, you can't do that.'

She raised one eyebrow at him. 'Oh?' Then she gave him her sweetest smile. 'I think you'll find that I can.'

His lean face became thunderous at that, and his whole body seemed to tense. He opened his mouth and shut it again. Then suddenly he put his hand up, rubbed it along the back of his neck, and stared fixedly down at the floor.

When he raised his head to face her again, his fury seemed to have dissipated like magic. He gave her a calm, thoughtful look, then in one swift movement he turned, shifted his weight up to perch on her desk, his long legs dangling over the edge, and before she could collect herself enough to object, calmly took out a cigarette from his shirt pocket and lit it.

Blowing out smoke, he smiled crookedly at her. 'Come on, now, Professor,' he said in a silky, confidential tone. 'I think if we put our heads together we can work this thing out amicably. A little give and take.' He waved his cigarette in her direction. 'You know?'

Claire brushed away the smoke that stung her eyes and glared at him. 'First of all, I am not a professor, I am only a teaching assistant.'

'Well, whatever,' he said blithely, with another airy wave. 'What difference does it make?'

'It makes a great deal of difference, as it happens. It's up to Professor Gregg whether to pass or fail your football player. All I do is grade the tests.'

He flashed her a broader smile, which was obviously intended to disarm her completely. 'Yes, but he'll have to rely on the grade you give to make that decision, won't he?'

'Probably,' she replied curtly. 'That's the usual procedure.'

'Then I'll just have to persuade you to change the grade, won't I?'

'I'm afraid that won't be possible. Scott not only hasn't the slightest conception of the material we've been studying, he also doesn't have the remotest interest in it. I cannot in conscience pass a student with that kind of record.'

'Why not?'

'Well, it wouldn't be fair to the others, for one thing, the ones who have really worked hard for their grades.'

'Don't worry about that. I'll take care of it. Take my word for it, most of your students would far rather be treated unfairly in an English course than have to suffer through another losing football season. Anything else?' He slid off the desk and looked around for an ashtray.

Claire crossed around to the front of the desk, opened the top drawer, and pulled out a chipped pottery saucer. She shoved it towards him with a jerk. By now she was so angry she could barely speak.

'Mr Donovan,' she said in a voice throbbing with suppressed rage, 'I don't think you quite understand my position here.'

'I'm trying.' He flicked ash into the dish and gave her a polite, expectant look.

'Then let me explain to you how I deal with cases like this one. If I see any glimmer at all of a genuine desire to learn, I'll give the student every chance. I'll arrange for special tutoring, even take on the job myself.' She paused and looked at him.

'Go on. I'm listening.'

She took a deep breath. 'I try to reserve judgement and to be fair, but if I become convinced that the student is merely looking for an easy passing grade, I have no mercy. He gets the grade he deserves, and that's that.'

It was all true. In the two years she had been working as a teaching assistant at Rainier College while she finished her doctoral dissertation, she'd learned the hard way how important it was to be firm with her students, most of whom were only two or three years younger than she was. She couldn't afford to let them walk all over her just because she was so young, yet she strove constantly for objectivity and fairness.

While she spoke, he had been slowly grinding out his cigarette in the pottery saucer, staring down intently at the mess he was making. When she was through, he raised his head and folded his arms across his chest.

'Well, it's not going to be like that this time,' he said in a low tone of utter conviction.

'What do you mean?'

'Are you going to give Scott a passing grade or not?'

'No. I just got through telling you. I can't do that.'

He nodded once abruptly, then crossed directly in front of her and strode towards the door. He pushed it open and stepped out into the corridor without a backward glance.

Claire stood there staring after him until he disappeared from view around a corner. When he was gone, her right hand rose involuntairly to her throat as she listened to his firm footsteps echoing in the empty halls, a sinking feeling in a pit of her stomach.

Somehow she had a feeling the issue was far from settled. In fact, she was quite certain she had by no means heard the last of Jake Donovan.

'Well Claire, how are things going with you?' Kate asked at dinner that night. 'Still plugging away at good old Rainier College?'

Claire jumped. As the quietest member of the group of women who were meeting that evening for their regular Thursday dinner, she always tried to avoid the spotlight. As usual, she'd remained silent throughout most of the meal at the interesting little Vietnamese restaurant Kate had chosen. It was her turn, and she always came up with a novelty, as yet undiscovered by Seattle's contingent of Yuppies.

Claire glanced at her now, her mind trying to form a response to the well-worn, polite question. Somehow, here in the busy restaurant with its exotic smells, the loud sounds of clattering crockery and shouted orders, all her affairs seemed so trivial, and it came to her just how dull her life must seem to the rest of them.

Still, she had to say something. The purpose of these weekly meetings was to keep the friends abreast of what was going on in each other's lives on a regular basis, and Claire was a little embarrassed by the fact that she never had anything to contribute that even remotely interested the others. Since their main concern in life and virtually sole topic of conversation seemed to be men, while her own interests were firmly concentrated on her work, she understood and accepted that she was doomed to be odd woman out in these gatherings.

Kate, the psychologist among them and Claire's closest friend, was still watching her expectantly, waiting for her to say something. Grasping at the first straw that came to mind, and still smarting from her unpleasant encounter with Jake Donovan that afternoon, she decided she might as well tell her about it.

'Well, there is one thing,' she said slowly. A rather unsettling experience, in fact. This afternoon I got some heat from the football coach about one of my flunking athletes.'

Kate's eyes flew open, and she bent her head closer. 'The football coach?' she asked breathlessly. 'You mean Jake Donovan?'

Claire nodded.

'Wow!' Kate breathed. 'That's a lot of man! A real

hunk!'

'Do you know him?'

'Only by reputation, I'm afraid. Tell me what happened.'

Claire went on to describe the interview she'd had with Scott and the later appearance of the belligerent coach, who definitely came out second-best in the telling of it.

'In fact,' she finished indignantly, 'he's got to be the most arrogant, overbearing, conceited man I've ever met!'

'That's too bad,' Kate commented thoughtfully. 'When you first mentioned him, I was hoping you'd met a real man at last.

Just then a dark, short-haired girl across the table snorted loudly. 'Are you kidding? We all know the man doesn't exist who can turn Claire on.'

Claire looked around, red-faced, to find all six pairs of eyes firmly fixed on her. Apparently the others had been listening with undisguised interest to her impassioned recitation.

'Come on, Deirdre,' Claire protested. 'That's not fair.'

'Oh, really?' Kate put in. 'We've all been trying since high school to come up with likely prospects for you, and you turn your nose up at every one of them.' She sighed. 'It's those blasted books of yours.'

'Books?' Claire asked, puzzled. 'What have books got to do with it?'

Kate waved a hand in the air. 'Oh, you know. All those dark, enigmatic heroes. You'd rather read abut Heathcliff tramping across the moors or poor Mr

Rochester than deal with a real man.'

Claire forced out a smile, yet she was squirming inside at Kate's probing dissection of her character, which, she had to admit, came uncomfortably close to the truth. 'And just what do you call Curtis Gregg?' she asked coolly.

'Oh, Curtis,' Kate said with a wave of her hand that clearly dismissed the head of the English department from the category of real men. 'He's just your boss.'

Claire was about to tell her that Curtis was much more to her than just a boss when the smiling Vietnamese waiter came to the table with their after-dinner coffee, silencing any further discussion for the moment. While he poured out the steaming liquid, Claire sat back in her chair and mentally detached herself from the rest of the group.

Kate's remarks about her non-existent love-life and the reason behind it had stung her, and she was sorry now she'd ever brought up the subject of Jake Donovan. Was it true? Had she retreated into a world of fictional heroes simply to avoid involvement with real men?

A familiar, half-forgotten ache of sadness began to tug at her heart. No, she thought unhappily, it wasn't true. In the hidden recesses of her being she still longed for love, still even nursed the faint hope that she might find it with Curtis, no matter what Kate thought of him. So what if he'd only been able to stir a tepid response in her? So far he hadn't tried very hard, and although she'd begun to wonder secretly if much passion existed in Curtis Gregg, there was still a chance that that could change in time.

As soon as the waiter was gone, Kate cleared her throat, leaned towards Claire and fixed her with her most intense, professional stare. 'I think we'd better forget Curtis and get to the bottom of this problem you're having with Jake Donovan. Surely the news has seeped through even into your ivory tower that he's Rainier College's Great White Hope?'

Claire stared blankly at her. 'I don't know what you're talking about. He's only a football coach.'

Kate set her coffee-cup down hard. 'Honestly, Claire, I don't believe you sometimes! I know you hate football, but you'd have to live in a cave not to know that, before he retired from the game, Jake Donovan was probably the greatest quarterback in recent football history. Do you know what a quarterback is?'

'Of course I do,' replied Claire indignantly. 'He's the one who decides whether to throw the ball to another player or run with it himself for a touchdown.'

Kate nodded. 'That's close enough. The important point is that he's the brains of the whole outfit. All the other players on his team are out there mainly to protect him.'

'I get the picture,' Claire said drily.

'Now, Donovan was smarter than most professional players. He retired early, about five years ago, at the peak of his powers. He'd already made a bundle from endorsement and franchises, plus his astronomical salary. It think he was only about thirty at the time, and he still had five or six good years in him.'

'Why did he do that if he was making all those piles

of money? That doesn't sound so smart to me,' Claire retorted.

Kate tapped the side of her head. 'As I said, brains, that's why. From what I hear, he's a shrewd investor who now only needs to sit around and count his money.'

'Then what's he doing coaching at Rainier College?'

'Charity, my dear. Sweet charity. That's why he's the blue-eyed boy. Rainier happens to be his *alma mater.*'

Claire made a face. 'I suppose he got shoved through his courses just as he wants me to do with Scott.'

'Not on your life. He got a special commendation in business. and was top of his graduating class.'

'And you say he's coaching here at Rainier for free?'

'That's right.' Kate eyed her carefully. 'Come on now, Claire, admit it. You just hate football. With Jake Donovan at Rainier, the school finally has a chance for a winning season. They've beaten the University of Puget Sound and Seattle Pacific already this season, for the first time in ten years, and the graduates' association is going wild.'

'And what about academic integrity?' Claire enquired loftily.

'Did you see that game with UPS last Saturday?' put in a thin blonde. 'What a rout that was!'

A heated discussion of the relative merits of the two teams ensued, and Claire sat quietly drinking her coffee while the argument raged around her. Although they could have been speaking a foreign language for all the sense it made to her, she was relieved at no longer being expected to respond. She didn't particualarly enjoy hearing her ignorance of a stupid game analysed as though it was some kind of disease they were all trying to cure her of.

With half her mind she listened to the argument which was definitely escalating now, and with the other she glanced idly into the large plate-glass window just to her left.

It was so dark outside that the window appeared to have a solid black backing. The bright lights inside the restaurant falling on it made it into a sort of mirror, and Claire could see their reflections in it quite clearly.

We're all so different, she thought. We always have been. We haven't really changed since we were little girls just starting school. She eyed her own reflection critically. Taller than the others, with a sturdy bone-structure, she looked, she decided, rather solid and a little boring. Not pretty like Barbara; not interesting like Deirdre; not efficient little Kate.

Her thick, dark auburn hair was braided into two heavy ropes coiled at the top of her head, and she habitually wore suits, almost always grey or brown shades, all in an effort to appear older than her twenty-four years. Besides, she believed her colouring was too dramatic for anything but neutral tones, with her tawny eyes and gleaming reddish hair.

Her mind began to wander, and she thought about her doctoral dissertation, almost entirely researched now. Next would come the drafting, the revisions, and she should be able to finish it by spring. Once she received the coveted doctorate degree, her academic future would be secure.

'Claire!' It was Kate's piercing voice, a little shrill with annoyance.

Claire turned and gave her a guilty look. 'Sorry, Kate,' she apologised. 'I guess I was wool-gathering.'

'You're the only person I know, Claire Talbot, who gets bored when you're the main topic of conversation.' Kate frowned at her. 'I can't help wondering why. It's not normal.'

Claire raised her hands in a helpless gesture. 'It's just that I'm so dull,' she said with a smile. 'Now, if you want to talk about my dissertation or my classes, you'll have a hard time shutting me up.'

'We were discussing your problem with Jake Donovan,' Kate said severely. 'The majority opinion is that you should give his star player a passing grade.'

Claire shrugged. 'Well,' she hedged, 'I'll think it over very carefully.' Shrewdly, she changed the subject. 'How are you and Harold getting along?'

Harold and Kate had been experimenting with their marriage since the day of the wedding. As Claire had anticipated, Kate immediately warmed to her favourite subject, giving her a bright smile and launching into an involved discussion of their latest crisis.

Later that night, in the bedroom of her tiny apartment just off campus, Claire stood in front of her mirror in her nightgown, brushing out her hair and thinking over the evening's conversation.

In spite of Kate's glowing accolade on the superior

qualities of Mr Jake Donovan, to Claire, more was at stake here than satisfying a graduates' association's cherished hopes for a winning football team, especially if it meant catering to the ego of that arrogant man.

It was a matter of principle. If she compromised her integrity over this issue and did what he asked, changed Scott's grade so that he'd pass the course, where would it end? The track star would be next. She couldn't do it. She *wouldn't* do it!

She put her brush down, struck suddenly by Kate's derogatory comments about Curtis Gregg. Granted, he was no romantic hero; still, he was a kind, gentle, sensitive man. They had a lot in common, and she felt safe with him. He never made demands on her. He understood her dedication to her work. He . . .

She paused, frowning. Why was she making excuses for Curtis? She made a face at her reflection. With her uninteresting looks, what did she expect?

Yet she really wasn't bad-looking, she thought, posing a little. Although her frame was large, she hadn't an ounce of excess flesh. It must be her attitude. Leering slightly, she practised a sultry, come-hither look. She broke out laughing at the comical spectacle she made, switched off the light and got into bed.

Later, as she drifted off to sleep, her last thought was that with luck, by tomorrow the silly problem with Jake Donovan would be resolved. As head of her department, Curtis would surely back her up, and that would be the end of it.

By the next afternoon, Claire had half forgotten the whole episode. Scott hadn't been in class that day, and she hoped that meant he and his coach had taken her decision as final.

She had just settled down at her desk to continue grading the mid-term exams when there was a light knock on the door and Curtis Gregg came into her office.

She looked up from her desk and smiled at him. 'I'll bet you're looking for these,' she said, holding up the remaining ungraded papers. 'I should finish them by Monday if I take them home over the weekend.'

Curtis nodded absently. He was a slightly built, rather stooped man, and dressed in the academic's traditional uniform of baggy tweeds, coloured shirt, knitted tie and argyle-patterened sweater, none of which matched. A briar pipe was clenched between his teeth, and his jaunty beard, moustache and gently receding hairline were all of a nondescript greying colour.

'Actually,' he said, removing the dead pipe and tucking it in his jacket pocket, 'I came to discuss something else.' He walked over to the window, pulled the dingy curtain aside, and gazed down at the campus grounds below.

After a moment, Claire said lightly, 'Nothing serious, I hope?'

He turned around. 'I hope so, too. It seems our football coach has been making waves about the grade you gave Scott Cunningham in his mid-term exam.'

Claire stiffened. Although Curtis's tone was half-joking, she could sense a hidden undercurrent of faint disapproval in it.

'I see,' she said quietly.

Curtis shrugged and came to stand in front of her desk, leaning over, his hands braced on the edge. 'I just want you to know that I understand your position perfectly and am in complete sympathy with the stand you've taken in the matter.'

Claire's stomach muscles unclenched and she breathed a sigh of relief. 'I'm very glad to hear that, Curtis,' she said.

'Furthermore, I find it absolutely disgusting that any of us should have to put up with that kind of harassment in a supposedly free academic community.' His moustache twitched as he wrinkled his nose in distaste.

'I couldn't agree more. That's why . . .'

Curtis raised a hand. 'On the other hand, we must tread warily here. The football programme brings in a lot of money to the school, and you know how these sports freaks put men like Donovan on a pedestal. What you may not know, however, is that he's coaching the team for free.'

'I did hear something to that effect,' she said in a tight voice.

'And so, I too have had pressure put on me—by President Carlisle, no less—to try to change your mind.'

Claire went quite still. 'Curtis,' she said at last, 'are you telling me you want me to lie about Scott's grade?'

His pale blue glance flicked her way without quite meeting her eyes. 'No,' he said slowly. 'I'm not asking you to do that.'

'Well, thank goodness for that!' she exclaimed with feeling.

'I did, however, promise the president that I would put it to you that if there is any hope at all for the boy, any possibility that with a little special help he might be able to pass a re-sit test, he would greatly appreciate it.'

Claire got up and began to pace around the tiny room. 'Curtis,' she said at last, wheeling around to face him, 'I honestly don't see a shadow of promise in Scott Cunningham. In my estimation, he's beyond hope.' She frowned. 'But there's one thing I don't understand. Whether he passes or fails the course is really up to you in the end. I only grade the tests. If you want to pass him there's nothing stopping you.'

'Ah, but there is. You forget that those grades are all part of the official record. If he has indeed failed every exam, I couldn't very well pass him, could I?'

'You could regrade the test, I suppose,' she said slowly. 'If it's really important to you.'

He drew himself up and looked down his nose at her. 'I hope you're not suggesting that I would falsify a test score, Claire, or implying that your ideals are somehow nobler or higher than my own.'

'Oh, of course not, Curtis. I guess I just don't like the way all the responsibility for this thing is dumped on me.' She knotted her fingers together and added in a tight voice, 'I wish it would just go away.'

'A pretty empty hope, I'm afraid. I know Donovan. He won't give up without a fight, and he carries a tremendous amount of weight with the graduates' association.'

Claire gazed at him thoughtfully for several seconds. Then she said quietly, 'Curtis, what do you want me to do?'

'Nothing, for now. I told the president I'd look into the matter as head of the English department. I've done so. Now I'll report back to him, and the ball will be in his court.'

'What will you say?'

He came over and put an arm around her shoulders. 'Just that my bright young teaching assistant is a woman of the hightest integrity and totally incorruptible.'

She smiled up at him. 'Thanks, Curtis. It helps to know you're backing me.'

He gave her a little squeeze. 'I'll let you get back to work now,' he said, and started walking away from her. At the door he turned and raised one hand in a farewell salute. Then, as an afterthought, he added, 'By the way, if you can finish grading those papers before the weekend, I'll take you to dinner Saturday night as a reward.'

'Well, with that kind of incentive, I'll certainly do my best,' she replied.

Then he turned around and went off down the hall.

It was after six o'clock and growing dark when Claire finally finished. Yawning hugely, she stretched her arms wide and flexed her cramped fingers. Done at last! Curtis would be pleased.

She straightened the papers on her desk neatly, then got up to close the curtains. It was not only dark out, but a light rain had begun to fall. She only had to walk a few blocks to her apartment, and luckily she had brought a raincoat that morning.

She slipped on her coat, turned off the light and went out into the corridor, deserted at this hour except for a lone caretaker, who was lazily pushing a wide broom back and forth up at the far end of the corridor.

She had just bent over to put the key in the lock when she heard footsteps coming towards her from behind. She straightened up instantly, but before she could turn round to see who it was, a strong hand had gripped her upper arm hard, forcing her around until she came face to face with a patently furious Jake Donovan.

His dark hair was wet from the rain, there was an unshaven stubble on his hard lean cheeks, and his glittering green eyes were fixed on her as though she were some specimen of plague bacteria which he intended to wipe out on the spot.

He grabbed her other arm and actually shook her a little. 'I want to talk to you,' he ground out.

'You're hurting me!' she cried.

'Good,' he snarled, then kicked open the office door and shoved her bodily inside.

CHAPTER TWO

'JUST what am I going to have to do, Miss Talbot, to persuade you to see things my way? Break your neck?'

Once inside the door, Jake had slammed it shut with a loud bang that reverberated throughout the empty building. Released at last from that punishing grip, Claire found herself being slowly backed into a corner of the room. Finally he stopped and stepped back a few paces, while she stood there, literally speechless with fury and rubbing her arms where his strong fingers had bitten into them.

'I've tried reason,' he went on in a sanctimonious tone, spreading his arms wide to indicate his frustration. 'I've tried gentle pressure through what's his name—the guy with the beard. Jiggs, is it?'

'Gregg!' she sputtered. 'His name is Curtis Gregg, and he happens to be . . .'

He held up a hand to silence her. 'Whatever. It doesn't matter what his name is. Apparently he had no more influence over you than I did. You'd think he could control his own people better that that.' He eyed her severely. 'Now, are you going to co-operate—for the good of the team, which means the good of the school, and, I might add, for the good of your skin—or am I going to have to call out some heavy artillery?'

In the meantime, Claire was struggling to fight down the unpleasant combination of rage and physical fear that seemed to have a stranglehold on her throat muscles. When she finally realised he didn't intend to do her actual bodily harm, the fury took over to the point where she seriously wondered if she'd ever be able to speak again.

While she stood there opening and closing her mouth in an effort to choke out the epithets forming on her tongue, he stood before her, an expectant look on his face, his hands in his trouser pockets jingling keys and change, just as though they were having a normal discussion about the weather.

Finally she found her voice, a little hoarse, but still a voice. 'I have no idea how you operate in your locker-room, if that's what it's called,' she said in a low, quivering tone, 'but these strong-arm tactics won't work with me. In fact, if there ever was a chance I might give in to your ridiculous—and, I might add, highly dishonourable—demands, you've just blown it by the way you manhandled me just now.'

His dark eyebrows shot up. 'Manhandled you? For God's sake, all I did was give you a gentle shove.'

'Gentle?' she cried. 'You call that gentle?' She could hear herself spluttering again, and made herself count to ten slowly in an effort to gain control of her emotions. 'At any rate,' she said at last, 'I wouldn't do what you wanted me to do now for anything on earth; not for the blasted team, not for the school, not even for my job. In fact,' she finished triumphantly, 'not for a million dollars.'

She raised her head and looked down her nose at him, daring him to do his worst. He could kill her on the spot, she vowed silently, before she'd budge an inch. They stood there for several seconds glaring at each other. Claire met his gaze unflinchingly, determined not to give way. Her eyelids felt like sand-paper and her jaw muscles were growing numb from clenching her teeth, but she would not give way.

Finally, he frowned and looked down at his feet, rubbing one hand thoughtfully along his jawline. In the silence of the room, Claire could hear the gentle rasping sound it made, the patter of the rain against the window, the thudding of her own heart.

After a moment or two, he raised his head and, to her utter amazement, smiled broadly at her. 'You're a tough nut to crack, do you know that, Miss Talbot?'

As the quick rush of intense relief washed over her, she was finally able to blink and relax her jaw. 'I only want to do what's right,' she said quietly.

He merely gazed at her for some time, still standing a few feet away from her. Then, suddenly, he took a step towards her, and as he came closer, still smiling, she stepped back from him until finally she came smack up against the wall. He stopped then, directly in front of her, and reached out a hand as though to touch her arm.

When she flinched, he immediatedly dropped it at his side. 'Did I really hurt you?' he asked softly.

'Yes, as a matter of fact you did,' she said sulkily. She looked up at him. She'd worn flat heels today, and the way he towered over her was still a little intimidating. Yet the smile made him seem much more human. In fact, he had a very nice smile. His mouth was thin, but his teeth were white and even against his dark skin, and the hard light was gone from his eyes.

'Let me make it up to you,' he said in the same low voice. 'Let me buy you dinner.'

This time, when he reached out a hand, she didn't shrink back, but allowed him to touch her lightly on the arm. The large hand began to move up and down her sleeve in a soothing, rhythmic motion, and she gazed up at him, open-mouthed, breathing a little hard, wondering what was going on, but lulled by the gentle pressure on her arm and the hypnotic green gaze.

'Dinner?' she croaked at last.

He took her by the elbow and began propelling her towards the door. 'Right. We'll go to that little Italian place on Lake Union and watch the boats out on the water. Have a few drinks, some cannelloni, and discuss this affair in a more civilised manner.'

She yanked her arm away immediately. 'I see,' she said, backing away from him and putting her hands on her hips. 'Wine me and dine me, then get me to do exactly what you want. You've got some nerve, Mr Donovan! Just who do you think I am?'

He stared down at her for a long time. At her words, the smile had vanished. His lips were set now in an straight, unyielding line. Finally, he shrugged and moved away from her towards the door.

'OK,' he said. 'Have it your way. I don't care. Believe me, I'll get what I want in the end. I always do.' His mouth twisted in a parody of a smile and his eyes raked her up and down. 'Too bad, though. Who knows? We might have had a good time. You look as if you could use a little thawing out.'

When he was gone, Claire stood in the silent room trembling with anger, her eyes shut tight, her hands clenched into fists and her arms rigid at her sides. But by the time his last footstep had fallen away, the anger was gone, and to her utter astonishment she suddenly felt the prick of hot tears behind her eyelids.

The next day was Saturday at last, and that night Claire drove to the small Greek restraurant in West Seattle to meet Curtis for the dinner he had promised her. Since he had a meeting in Tacoma that afternoon, they had arranged to make their own way there. It was a popular place with the college crowd, not too expensive, but with a wonderful selection of *moussaka*, *dolmathes*, *baklava* and other Greek delicacies.

When they were seated in the dining-room overlooking Puget Sound, the lights of the city and the harbour winking against the blue-blackness of the sky and water, Claire launched immediately into a description of her latest confrontation with Jake Donovan.

'Can you believe the gall of the man?' she exclaimed when she was through. 'The utter nerve! And then to have the insolence to assume that charming me over dinner would work where his threats had failed!'

Curtis allowed her to rave on unchecked, listening thoughtfully and alternately sipping his *ouzo* and chewing on his pipe. He would shake his head occassionally or nod, whichever seemed called for, but had remained silent throughout the entire impassioned recitation.

When she finally ran down, he leaned back in his chair, fixed her with a rather paternal eye, and heaved a deep, sorrowful sigh.

'I know how you must feel,' he said in a soothing tone. 'And believe me, I sympathise with you entirely.' He shook his head sadly. 'It must be terrible for a girl like you to be treated as a mere sex object, especially by a man like Jake Donovan.'

Terrible? Claire thought. Sex object? She frowned. 'That's not the point, Curtis. You don't understand. I don't think sex was on his mind for one second. If anything, with his perverted ego, he's probably convinced he's the sex object, not me. I think he actually expected me to be grateful for the opportunity.'

'Oh, come now, Claire. It can't have been as bad as that.'

She looked away. 'You weren't there, Curtis.'

He reached across the table to cover one of her hands with his and gave it a comforting squeeze. She turned back to him and smiled weakly.

'I guess I might have been over-reacting a little,' she said sheepishly. 'I just hate to be made a fool of.'

'That's better. Now, have you decided what you'd like for dinner?'

She sighed. 'I'm not terribly hungry, to tell you the truth.'

'Come on, now. A nice Greek salad, a glass of wine, some pitta bread, and you'll feel much better.'

The plump, smiling waitress came to the table just

then, and Curtis ordered for them both, his voice loud, confident and a trifle pedantic, his Greek pronunciation perfect.

When the waitress had gone, he turned back to Claire. 'Well, then, what have you decided to do?'

She gazed blankly at him. 'What do you mean?'

'I mean, about Jake Donovan.'

'I thought that was all decided. I'm not going to do anything.'

'Do you think that's wise?'

Claire frowned. 'Curtis, we've been all over this. You said you would back me, that you were behind whatever decision I made.'

He leaned forward, and took her hand in his. 'There is a way out, you know. A way that would satisfy everybody.'

'Why do we need to satisfy everybody?' she challenged, drawing her hand away.

Curtis straightened in his chair and gave her a severe look. 'Listen, Claire, if you want to get anywhere in the academic world, in any world, for that matter, you've got to learn the art of compromise.' She started to speak, but he held up a hand. 'Let me finish. There is a way, as I said, to keep everybody happy.'

'I'm listening.'

He smiled with satisfaction. 'All you have to do is arrange for Scott to get some special tutoring. Then, when you think he's up to it, give him a re-sit exam.' He shrugged. 'Not too difficult, of course. What we want here is to pass the idiot without compromising our own integrity.'

Claire had a hundred arguments against such a proposition, but something in the tone of Curtis's voice warned her that anything she said now would only be a waste of time. Clearly his mind was made up.

At the same time she had a pretty good idea why he was taking such a firm stand, and her respect for him fell a notch or two. Obviously, Jake Donovan had seen to it that more pressure had been put on him, and he'd buckled under it.

'You're very young, Claire,' he was saying now. 'And you have very high standards. Perhaps a little too high. You don't want to jeopardise a fine career all for the sake of one stupid athlete.'

'They got to you, too, didn't they, Curtis?' she asked quietly.

His pale eyes flew open, then narrowed. 'If you mean they convinced me they had a valid point in their favour,' he said stiffly, 'then yes, you could say that. It doesn't matter. Just do it, Claire. As a personal favour to me, or as a direct order, whichever you choose. But do it.'

She nodded. 'Of course. If you put it that way, then of course I'll do it.' Maybe he was right. Maybe she was being too unyielding.

'Good.' He reached out for her again, but she quickly put both her hands in her lap.

'Here comes our dinner,' she said.

Over their meal the conversation was of more neutral subjects: other problems in the English department, Claire's doctoral thesis and her chance to get a coveted tenure job at Rainier, even Curtis's two children by a former marriage, and by tacit agreement there was no further talk at all of Scott Cunningham or Jake Donovan.

Yet it was still on Claire's mind. As she watched Curtis and listened to him speak, he seemed a different person to her, as though he had suddenly changed in a fundamental way. Or at least her perception of him had altered, and she was seeing him with new eyes. She'd always thought of him as a strong man, a fearless upholder of justice and integrity. Tonight he had revealed an aspect of himself she'd never dreamed existed, given in to a pressure she herself had determined to resist to the death, if necessary.

To her dismay, the one thought that kept cropping up in her mind, even as she spoke of other matters, was that you'd never see a man like Jake Donovan back down from a fight that way.

'Would you like an after-dinner drink?' Curtis asked her when they'd finished eating. He glanced at his watch. 'Although it will have to be a quick one. I promised Carol I'd pick up the boys tonight and keep them with me until Monday.'

Claire was just about to refuse when she heard someone call her name. She looked up to see Kate and Harold Dawson descending on their table.

'Well!' Kate cried in her usual carrying tones. 'Look who's here! Hi, Claire.' Then she looked down at Curtis. 'Hello, Curtis,' she said, with a marked air of condescension. 'How are you?'

Curtis rose to his feet. 'Quite well, thank you,' he replied stiffly.

Kate turned back to Claire. 'If you're through with dinner, why not join us in the bar for a drink?'

Curtis cleared his throat loudly. 'As a matter of fact, I was just about to leave,' he said. He looked at Claire. 'You have your own car, Claire. Stay with your friends, if you like.'

Her glance shifted from Curtis to Kate. She was well aware that there was no love lost between them, and ordinarily she would have left when he did, but tonight, still smarting under his inauspicious capitulation, she felt a little perverse.

'All right,' she said, getting up. 'I think I will.'

Curtis bowed stiffly, nodded at Harold, then turned on his heel and stalked off.

'Well!' Kate said. 'What's eating him?'

'Nothing,' Claire replied shortly. 'Come on, I could use that drink.'

They went up the three steps into the crowded cocktail-lounge next to the dining-room. It was quite dark inside, with music playing softly in the background, the familiar clink of glasses, muted conversations and an occasional burst of loud laughter. Harold found a table for them over in a corner near the bar, and they sat down.

'Honestly, Claire,' Kate said as soon as they were settled, 'I don't know what you see in that wimp.'

Claire smiled. It was an old, familiar argument. 'Oh, Curtis is all right.'

'Well, you could do a lot better than that for yourself if you'd only loosen up and . . .'

She broke off and turned to her husband, who had started complaining loudly about the service, and they immediately became embroiled in a heated argument on the subject of his serious impatience problem.

While they wrangled, Claire glanced around the dim, smoke-filled room, wishing she were anywhere but here and wondering why she'd agreed to come. As her eyes became accustomed to the darkness, her gaze was caught by a blonde woman sitting alone at the far end of the bar, and she wondered what she was doing there all by herself.

Probably looking for company, Claire decided. She seemed like the type: the elaborately sculptured hairdo, the thick make-up, the low-cut black dress. A cigarette dangled from her fingers as she surveyed the room through heavy-lidded, calculating eyes.

As Claire stared, fascinated, there was a sudden lull in the marital squabble across the table, and in the silence a familiar voice came from the direction of the bar, which was only a few feet away. Claire swivelled her head slightly in that direction to make sure, and immediately her worst fears were confirmed. There, perched casually on a bar stool, a drink in his hand, his head turned in profile, was Jake Donovan.

She drew in a sharp breath and turned quickly away. She was in no mood to do further battle with that man tonight. She only hoped he hadn't recognised her. And even if he had, what difference did it make? She'd have to face him sooner or later in all her ignominious defeat ready to eat whatever humble pie he wanted to shove her way.

He was with a group of three of four other men—more dumb athletes, Claire thought disgustedly.

Although her back was firmly turned away, she was still close enough to hear their conversation, which consisted mainly of highly complimentary remarks about the blonde sitting alone at the far end of the bar.

'Come on, Donovan,' one of them said. 'Let's see you do your stuff.'

Jake murmured something Claire couldn't quite hear, but it was obviously negative, because one of the other men began goading him now. 'I'll bet you ten dollars you strike out, Donovan,' he said in a taunting tone. 'I know that gal, and she's too rich for your blood.'

Fascinated by now at this bit of masculine byplay, Claire couldn't resist a quick look out of the corner of her eye. As she watched, Jake slid off the stool and stood to face his adversary. 'Ten dollars?' he asked. 'You're on.'

He started ambling slowly towards the blonde. When he reached the end of the bar, he sat down on the empty stool beside her and beckoned to the barman. Although he hadn't once given the blonde a direct look, Claire could almost see the hidden messages passing between them as they surreptitiously sized each other up.

It wasn't until he was served that he turned towards her and spoke a few quiet words. The blonde smiled, looked down at her empty glass, then nodded, and Jake raised a hand to summon the barman again.

From then on it was no contest. Their heads bent closer and closer together while they drank, and when their glasses were empty, they both got off their stools at the same time and started walking towards the side entrance. They stopped there, and Jake leaned over to speak to her. Then he turned and sauntered back to join his friends, who were all goggling openly at him with undisguised admiration.

Claire, however, was mesmerised by the blonde, who continued to stand there patiently right where Jake had left her, smoking a cigarette, apparently anxiously awaiting his return. Claire could hardly believe her eyes. How stupid could a woman be, to fall for such an obvious pick-up from a man like that?

She turned back to Kate, who was watching the whole thing thoughtfully. Harold was gone, most likely in search of a waitress.

'The great man in action,' Kate murmured, with a nod towards the group of men clustered around Jake at the bar. 'That sight alone is worth the price of admission.'

'I think it's digusting,' Claire rejoined hotly. 'Did you see the way that blonde . . .?'

She broke off when she saw Kate's eyes widen and shift past her. A cold, tingling sensation began to travel up and down her spine. Somehow she knew.

'Good evening, Miss Talbot,' she heard him say in a smooth, silky voice.

She turned and looked up at him. He was smiling broadly, the even white teeth gleaming. With every instinct she possessed, Claire longed to smack that self-satisfied smirk off his face, and she might have, except for Kate, who she knew was taking in everything with open-mouthed fascination.

'Hello, Mr Donovan,' she said curtly.

'I just wanted to thank you,' he went on in the same

oily tone.

'Thank me for what?' she asked innocently.

'I understand our little problem has been resolved and that you've very kindly offered to tutor my boy so he can pass his English course.'

'My, news travels fast. I only just now agreed to do it. Reluctantly, I might add.'

'Ah, but somehow I knew you would in the end. I could tell the first time we met that you had a generous nature.'

Before she could think up a cutting response, he had flashed the smile briefly at Kate and turned on his heel. The last she saw of him, he and his blonde were arm in arm and moving fast through the side door.

'Wow!' Kate said with feeling. 'What was that all about?'

Claire turned around. 'Oh, you remember. I told you all about it at dinner the other night.'

Kate nodded. 'Oh, yes. The football player.'

'Well, he won,' Claire said with a helpless shrug. 'He got to the president of the college or the graduates' association, and they put the screws on Curtis.'

'Who immediately caved in,' Kate commented waspishly. 'I'm not surprised.'

'Oh, well, I guess it won't kill me.' She tried out a smile. 'Who knows? I might even be able to beat some appreciation of English Literature into that thick head.'

Harold came back with their drinks just then, and Claire was more than glad to drop the whole subject.

* * *

Half an hour later, Claire was ready to go home. Kate and Harold hadn't had their dinner yet, so she left alone. Harold offered to walk out to the car park with her, but she assured him there was no need. It was only a short distance and well-lit, with people coming and going all the time.

When she stepped outside into the cold drizzle, however, she had second thoughts. It was later than she'd realised, and much darker. In fact, the car park had been so crowded when she'd arrived that she'd had to park over on the side of the building in an area that looked particularly dark and forbidding to her now.

She paused for a moment beside the entrance, shivering, her hands in her jacket pockets. Maybe she should go back and get Harold after all. Then, telling herself not to be such a baby, she pulled her collar up to keep the damp off the back of her neck, and started walking briskly through the mist towards the corner of the building.

In stark contrast to the busy, noisy restaurant, it seemed eerily quiet out here. The only sounds to be heard were her high heels tapping on the wet pavement, some distant traffic noises, and the low, melancholy hoot of a foghorn out on the Sound.

When she came to the corner, she stopped for a second before plunging ahead into the darkness. She could barely see her car, a small red Toyota, parked right where she'd left it, about twenty yards away. If only it weren't so dark there! And so empty! Hers seemed to be the sole car left in the whole area.

Squaring her shoulders, she took a deep breath and marched forward, looking straight ahead, trying not to run. On the way, she fumbled in her bag for her key and held it tightly in her hand so that she'd be all ready when she got there. The walk seemed more like twenty miles than twenty yards, but she finally made it.

She unlocked the car door and opened it, checked the back seat as the light came on, then slid behind the wheel and punched down the door-latch firmly. Weak and relief, she laid her head back for a few moments until her pulse-rate had settled down.

'It's times like these I wish I smoked,' she muttered aloud.

Actually, she was feeling pretty proud of herself. She'd crossed some fairly dangerous terrain by herself with courage and dispatch, and most importantly, without the help of a man.

Buoyed up by her self-congratulations, she shoved the key in the ignition and turned it. Nothing happened. She pressed the accelerator and tried again. This time the engine choked a little, then sputtered out. She continued pumping, and before long the pungent odour of petrol filled the car. She'd flooded the engine.

'Calm down,' she said, fighting panic. 'Wait a full minute, then try again.'

This time there wasn't even a sputter, just an ominous grinding noise that confirmed her worst fears. The battery she'd been meaning to replace for months had gone dead. There was no way out of it. She'd just have to go back inside the restaurant and get Harold to come out and give her a jump-start.

Of all the things to happen, on top of everything

else! It just wasn't her day. More disgusted with herself than frightened now, she opened the car door and stepped outside. She'd done it once, she could do it again.

But before she'd gone two steps, she heard a faint rustling sound coming from behind her, catlike footsteps. She stopped cold, listening. In the next moment she felt a hand clamp tightly over her mouth and another one clawing at her front of her clothes.

'Make one sound,' a low guttural voice breathed into her ear, 'and I'll kill you.'

Terrified out of her wits, Claire blindly nodded her agreement, but the minute the pressure on her mouth slackened slightly, the scream that had been building up inside her burst forth, and she got out one good yell before the pressure was on her mouth again, yanking her head back. She heard the ripping sound of tearing material, then something hard came crashing into the side of her head.

Bright stars glittered before her eyes, then there was total blackness. She felt her body go limp, and she was falling, falling falling . . . The last thing she heard before she lost consciousness was a dim shout in the distance, the sound of running feet.

When she came to, she was lying on the pavement, soaking wet, with a terrible dull ache in her head. Everything hurt. Her first thought was that at least she wasn't dead, her second that she had to get on her feet. With a low moan she managed to climb to her knees.

Then, as her eyes began to focus again, she could

see two figures locked together on the pavement, just beyond her car, and it slowly dawned on her that they were fighting. There was a lot of heavy breathing, low, grunting sounds, a man's voice crying out in a shout of pain, then silence as one of them fell to the ground.

In a moment, the footsteps started coming towards her. She struggled to her feet, swaying a little from the painful hammering in her head. Her one aim was to get out of there before he reached her.

She turned around to run, but at her first step the blackness threatened again. She stumbled, could feel herself falling. Then a pair of arms grabbed her from behind, holding her up. In a panic, she opened her mouth to scream, but stopped short when she heard his voice.

'Claire? Are you all right? It's OK. You're safe now.'

As the powerful arms turned her gently around, she looked up to come face to face with Jake Donovan. His features were somewhat blurred in the dark, but there was no mistake. With a loud sob, she fell towards him, leaning against his chest. His arms tightened and held her close in a warm, protective embrace.

She stood there, limp with relief, shivering and gulping noisily, still hardly able to believe she was really safe, while he made soothing noises and patted her back until finally she was calmer and crying quietly into his shirt.

At last, sniffing loudly, she looked at him. 'Is he . . .? Where . . .?' she croaked.

'Don't try to talk,' he said. 'It's all taken care of.' He motioned with a backward jerk of his head. 'He'll be out like a light until the police get here. Are you all right? I mean . . .?'

His glanced flicked downwards, and when her gaze followed his she saw that the sleeve of her jacket was ripped half off and the bodice of her blouse torn open to reveal a lacy bra and a good portion of firm, full breast.

'Yes,' she said hastily, pulling on the tattered fabric in an effort to cover herself. I'm fine.'

His hand came up to smooth back the loosened hair that had fallen around her face, and he smiled crookedly at her. 'You don't look so fine.'

'No, really. I'm all right.'

'Still, you should let a doctor take a look at you.'

'No.' She shook her head. 'I'm not hurt, just a little shaken.'

'We'd better go back inside, then, and call the police before our friend over there wakes up.'

Just then, from the distance, came the wail of a siren. As it came closer, he lifted his head, listening. 'Sounds as if someone's already taken care of that.' He looked down at her. 'You'll have to talk to them, you know.'

The next thing she knew, he had picked her up and started carrying her towards the lighted parking area out in front. As they passed under a tall lamp post, she noticed a stream of bright red blood trickling down from a nasty cut on his forehead.

'Oh,' she said. 'You've been hurt.'

He laughed. 'It's just a scrape, nothing compared to

what happens to the quarterback in a football game when he gets dumped on behind the line of scrimmage.'

They were at his car now, a silvery-grey Mercedes. He set her gently on her feet, unlocked the door and helped her inside, just as the first police car came screeching into the driveway.

He straightened up and waved to them. 'Over here,' he called.

An hour later, she'd made her statement to a plain-clothes detective, her attacker had been aroused, handcuffed and shoved into the back of the police car, and they'd taken him away.

By then a crowd had gathered in front of the restaurant at all the commotion, Kate and Harold among them, and Claire dreaded the thought of having to face any of them in her battered, ragged condition, even her friends. Although her nerves were still raw, she was feeling much better now and thought she could probably make it home by herself, perhaps ask Jake to call a taxi for her.

Then, without a word, Jake slid in beside her, fired the engine and started driving away from the milling gawkers.

'Which way?' he said at the main street. 'Right or left?'

CHAPTER THREE

IT WASN'T until they were half-way to her apartment that Claire remembered the blonde. What had he done with her? She was dying to ask him, but couldn't quite get up the nerve.

She was still a little off-base anyway from the abrupt and decisive way he had simply driven her away from the restaurant with no polite preliminaries, and certainly no interest whatsoever in what *her* wishes might be in the matter.

She knew she was being ungrateful. He had done her an enormous service this evening, rescuing her from serious injury, almost certain rape, if not death itself. He was a man in the habit of taking charge. It was his way, and she had no right to be offended at it.

Besides, the poor man was hurt himself. He had refused medical treatment, just as she had herself, and during his interview with the police had merely pressed his handkerchief over his forehead to stanch the wound.

When they stopped at the next crossroads, she glanced over at him. Under the glow of the street-lights, she could see the blood seeping slowly down the side of his face. The cut had obviously opened again.

'You really should have had that head taken care of,'

she said.

He craned his neck forward, and took a quick look at his reflection in the rear-view mirror, frowning a little. Then the light changed, and he shifted the gears smoothly and shot forward. After a few seconds he darted a quick glance at her.

'You're one to talk,' he said, reaching over and pulling down her sun visor. 'Look at you. You're a mess.'

When she took a look at herself in the mirror on the underside of the visor, she could hardly believe her eyes. She didn't know whether to laugh or cry. Her thick braids had come unpinned and were hanging down over her shoulders, the area around her right eye was turning an ugly, mottled shade of blue, and her clothes were torn.

Finally she had to admit it really was rather funny. 'You're right,' she said, grinning at him.

He glanced at her again, and their eyes met briefly. 'We're quite a pair,' he said.

In a few minutes he turned into her street, and she pointed out her apartment building in the middle of the block. 'There it is,' she said.

He pulled over to the kerb, switched off the engine and turned to her. 'I'll see you to the door.'

'Oh there's no need . . .' she began, but by then he was out of the car.

He crossed in front of it, opened her door for her, and they walked up the path together, his hand lightly tucked beneath her elbow.

Since her apartment was on the ground floor, there were no steps to climb, and she wouldn't really need his help. She was feeling stronger by the minute, anyway, and all she really wanted was to get inside, have a long, hot soak in a bath and go to bed.

'Well, thank you again for coming to my rescue tonight,' she said at the entrance to the building. Then she noticed that he had the bloody handkerchief out again and was moping at his forehead. 'If you'd like to come in for a minute, I'll fix that up for you.'

'That's good of you,' he said politely.

They walked in silence down the hall. At her door, she took out her key and unlocked it. He followed her inside. It wasn't until she had switched on the light and they were standing together in her living-room that she began to wonder if it had been a very wise move to invite him in.

He seemed to fill the small room with his alien presence. She watched him with a growing sense of unease as he strolled around, very much at home, inspecting the books and papers stacked on her desk, the framed Picasso prints hanging on the wall, the needlepoint cushion on the couch.

Then, on an impulse, she said, 'By the way, what happened to the blonde?'

Now *that* got a reaction from him. He turned around slowly and gave her a long, suspicious look. 'What blonde?'

'Oh, come on. I was there. I saw the whole thing.' She took off her jacket and laid it on the back of a chair. 'None of my business, of course. I was just curious.'

To her astonishment, he turned an interesting shade of red then lifted his broad shoulders nonchalantly.

'That was just a bet,' he said in an offhand tone.

'I see. Something like a dare.'

'You could put it like that.'

'Do you always feel compelled to accept every challenge you're given?' she asked lightly.

'Not always.' He eyed her narrowly. 'Why the inquisition?'

'I was just curious.'

'Well you sound exactly like my third grade school-teacher. I'm beginning to have more and more sympathy for poor Scott.'

'Sorry about that. As I say, I was only wondering. I realise it's none of my business, but it seems to me there's another person involved here.'

He stared at her, uncomprehending. Then the light dawned. 'Oh, you must mean Shirley.'

'If that's her name.'

He waved a hand dismissively. 'Shirley and I are old pals. She did it as a favour to me.'

'I thought a gentleman never bet on a sure thing.'

'Who's claiming to be a gentleman? Besides, Shirley has a mind of her own.' He turned his back on her and started prowling around again. 'Say,' he said over his shoulder, 'you wouldn't have something around here to drink, would you?'

Then she remembered what he'd done for her tonight, at great risk to himself, and felt a little ashamed of putting him on the spot like that. Whatever she thought of his personal habits, she probably owed him her life.

'Of course,' she said quickly. 'But shouldn't we get that wound taken care of first?'

'I'd rather have the drink,' he said firmly. 'If you don't mind.'

'Up to you. Do you like wine?'

He made a face. 'Not if you've got Scotch or brandy.'

She thought a minute. She and Curtis only drank wine, but there was a bottle of brandy in the kitchen cupboard that she was saving for her father for Christmas.

'Right. I'll just be a minute.' She started walking towards the kitchen.

'And Claire . . .' he called after her. She turned around. 'Pour a glass for yourself, too. You look as though you could use it.'

'Oh, I'm perfectly all right now,' she said.

However, by the time she got to the kitchen and was reaching up into the cupboard for the bottle of brandy, the close call she'd had that night suddenly crashed into her mind in all its gruesome detail.

She could literally feel that hand pressing against her mouth, the fingers ripping at her clothes, the blow to her head, and a sickening wave of dizziness passed over her. She set the bottle down hard on the counter, leaning over it, her head down.

Soon she was shivering uncontrollably, her teeth chattering so loud she could hear them clicking together in the stillness of the room. Fighting hard for control, she braced her hands on top of the counter for support and hung her head lower.

The roaring in her head grew louder and louder, and she didn't even hear Jake's footsteps or realise he'd come up behind her until she felt his hands on her shoulders and heard his low voice at her ear.

'It's OK,' he said. 'Just reaction. Don't fight it. The sooner you let go, the sooner it will pass.'

He turned her to face him and put his arms around her, holding her close, and she sank gratefully up against him, trying to do what he said and relax. Finally, the trembling slowly subsided, and a great lassitude filled her whole body, turning all her bones and muscles to jelly.

She felt utterly spent. With a sigh, she laid her head on his shoulder and gave herself up to the warmth and strength of his hard body, his close embrace.

They stood that way for a long time, until little by little she began to feel better. Then gradually it dawned on her that the comforting stroke of his hands on her back and shoulders had begun to take on a slightly different, more intimate character. Her mind was still a little hazy, and she wasn't entirely clear about what was going on, but she did know that it felt wonderful.

The thought suddenly came to her that this was nothing like Curtis's chaste, tepid embraces. Although there had been a certain amount of affection between them, her relationship with Curtis had been far from passionate. But clearly this man meant business. There was deliberate intent and an iron determination, as well as a lot of skill, behind those stroking hands.

She really ought to stop him, she thought groggily, but it felt so good. The warmth that was coursing through her bloodstream seemed to be bringing her back to life again, and when he pressed her even closer she didn't have the energy or will to resist.

Then she felt his mouth on her hair, his soft breath in her ear. One large, warm hand was moving on her face now, slipping down over her chin to grasp her lightly around the neck and tilting her chin up until she was staring directly into those glittering green eyes. He's going to kiss me, she thought, and closed her eyes.

When his mouth finally came down on hers, it wasn't the demanding exploration she had expected at all, but a soft, almost tentative touch that only aroused a hunger for more. As though he sensed her response, his lips parted slightly, and the pressure increased. At this point she had no choice, no will of her own. All she could do was give herself up to the pleasure of the moment.

As the kiss deepened, she felt his other hand move around her waistband, slide slowly up over her stomach, her ribcage, until it came to settle on her breast. The warmth and strength of the intimate touch sent shock-waves through her, intensifying the heat that had already built up inside.

But when she felt his fingers slip inside her torn bodice to explore the bare flesh underneath, she suddenly came to her senses and wrenched her mouth away from his.

Still breathing hard, she stepped back a pace and put a hand to her throat, staring blankly at him. With a puzzled frown, he moved towards her, reaching out for her again. When she immediately stepped further back, he dropped his hands at his sides.

'What's wrong?' he asked quietly.

She ran a hand distractedly over her tangled hair and laughed nervously. 'Oh, nothing. Everything.' When she saw he wasn't laughing with her, she sobered. 'It's just the wrong place and the wrong time,' she said softly. 'Please try to understand.'

Still frowning, he opened his mouth to speak, but before he could say anything she went on briskly, 'Now, let's get that head of yours taken care of.'

He held up a hand. 'Wait a minute. Not so fast.' He reached out and grasped her firmly by the wrist. 'My head is fine. Now, I want to know what's going on here.'

He started pulling her towards him, but she dug in her heels. 'Let me go,' she said.

'Not until you tell me what's wrong.'

Annoyed at his commanding tone, she raised her head and gave him a defiant look. 'I've been mugged, assaulted and almost killed tonight, that's what wrong.'

He nodded. 'OK, I grant you that. But it didn't stop you a minute ago. That's not it and you know it.'

'Isn't that enough?' she cried. 'Now let me go.'

His eyes searched hers for several long, silent seconds, then, abruptly, he released her. 'You're lying,' he stated flatly, contempt in every syllable. 'Either to me or to yourself.'

He started moving towards the door. When he got there, he turned around. 'There's a word for women like you,' he said nastily, 'and it isn't very nice.'

'You've got some nerve!' she said. 'How dare you accuse me of anything? Just because you helped me out tonight doesn't give you the right to barge in here and—and—*attack* me.'

'Attack you?' he shouted. 'Is that what you call it? Come on, lady, you've got to do better than that.'

'Well, you took advantage of me when I . . .' She faltered and bit her lip as tears of self-pity welled up behind her eyes.

'Oh, no,' he said sternly. 'You can forget the tears. That damsel-in-distress routine won't work twice in one night.' He rested his knuckles on his lean hips and cocked his head. 'You know what I think?'

'I honestly don't care what you think,' she mumbled. 'I just want you to . . .'

'Well, I'll tell you anyway. I think you've become so used to hiding in your ivory tower and dealing with nice, safe men like that milk-and-water boss of yours that you're terrified of your own feelings.'

'I see. And you're the one who can save me from all that, I take it.'

'Who knows? You certainly seemed eager enough to give it a try a few minutes ago.'

She flushed deeply. 'That's not fair. You took advantage of me.' She lifted her chin. 'Now I'll tell you what I think. I think you've got a bad case of bruised ego, and you're only angry because I didn't fall panting at your feet tonight.'

His eyes widened in shocked disbelief. 'Are you kidding? Do you really think I'm so desperate that I'd waste any time worrying over an uptight college teacher who gets in a panic and backs off the minute thing begin to get interesting?' He gave a loud snort. 'Give me a break, lady.'

'Interesting? Is that what you call it?' She took a step towards him, then thought better of it when the green eyes began to glitter menacingly. 'I'm not one of your—your—*floozies*, you know.'

He raised an eyebrow and stared at her. 'Floozies? Listen, Miss Talbot, I'll take a floozy any day over a tease like you.'

'Get out,' she said in a low voice trembling with emotion. 'Just get out of here. Now.'

'With pleasure.' He wheeled around and stormed out, slamming the door loudly behind him.

When he was gone, still fuelled by her anger, Claire marched straight to the door, locked it and shot the chain-bolt firmly home. There was no telling what a man like that was capable of. She'd never in her life been subjected to such boorish behaviour.

She went to the bathroom and switched on the bright overhead light. When she peered at her reflection in the mirror and had her first clear view of what she looked like, she had to wonder just *why* he'd behaved that way. It wasn't just the tangled hair or the purple bruise or the torn, wet clothing that would have turned him off, although that was bad enough.

She simply wasn't the kind of woman men made passes at, not to mention men with the slick expertise in sexual sparring that Jake Donovan obviously had. Ever since school, when all her friends were fending off hot-blooded suitors, she'd had only a few mild fliratations that never went anywhere, and all with young men as dull and bookish as herself.

Men like Curtis Gregg, she added, bland, unthreatening men who were more interested in her mind than her body. She'd been too tall, too serious, too intelligent to attract the athletic heroes or the popular boys, and the polite version among her friends was that she preferred those quiet, studious men. She had fostered that fiction herself, both to them and to herself.

What her friends didn't realise, however, and what was only just now beginning to dawn on her, was that that was all it was: a fiction, a lie. The feelings Jake Donovan had awakened in her tonight could possibly be chalked up to her weakened condition after the ordeal with the mugger, but somehow she doubted it.

She could still feel the hard body pressed against hers, the taste of his demanding mouth, the seeking hands, the masculine smell of his hair and skin, clean and pungent, the rough feel of his jaw as it rasped against her cheek. Swaying a little at the vivid memory, she closed her eyes tight and put out a hand to steady herself on the wash-basin.

Then, slowly, she got undressed, brushed out her hair and pinned it up. She ran a hot bath and sank back gratefully into the comforting warmth. A good night's sleep was all she needed. Tomorrow was Sunday. The mid-term papers were all graded. She could lounge around all day and catch up on her reading.

But somehow that prospect didn't seem nearly as attractive to her as it used to. As she lay there soaking, she kept trying to work up some of her old indignation at Jake's rude behaviour, but memory kept intruding. The green eyes gleaming with desire, the sheer physical presence of the man, simply wouldn't go away.

In the end she decided it really didn't matter. The one thing certain was that he wouldn't try it again. A man like that, with his success rate and more than his share of male vanity, wouldn't be pleased at the way she'd rebuffed him.

First thing on Monday morning, Curtis came rushing into her office and came to stand over her desk, an anguished look on his face.

'My God, Claire!' he said. 'I only just found out what happened at the restaurant on Saturday night after I left. Are you all right?'

She took off her glasses, leaned back in her chair and looked up at him with amusment. 'Of course I am, Curtis. Can't you see that for yourself?'

He perched on the edge of her desk. 'I'll never forgive myself for leaving you like that. Never! Why, you could have been seriously injured. Raped! Murdered!'

'Well, I wasn't,' she assured him mildly. 'And all's well that ends well. I just want to forget about it.' Especially what happened afterwards, she added silently.

Yesterday she'd had one telephone call after another from her friends, all anxious to hear first-hand what had happened to her, and by now she was sick of the whole subject. Kate, in particular, had been annoyingly insistent in her demands for information about Jake's part in the whole affair. So far she'd been able to fend her off, but Kate wasn't one to be side-tracked so easily, and Claire knew she hadn't heard the end of it.

Then she realised that Curtis was still speaking, accusing himself, justifying his actions, and she was getting more than a little fed up with that, too.

'Curtis, I already told you I'm perfectly all right. It wasn't your fault. How were you to know it would happen?'

'Well, I feel terrible that I didn't even find out about it until this morning. I was gone all day yesterday, took the boys up to Stevens Pass, camping, and didn't get home until late. It seems to me you could at least have called and let me know.'

'How could I, Curtis, when you were gone all day?'

'Did you even try?'

'Of course I did.'

'Well, that's all right, then.' He peered owlishly at her over his glasses. 'The story I heard was that Donovan interfered.'

'Interfered?' she asked drily. 'He only saved my life, that's all. If he hadn't come along when he did, I hate to think of what might have happened.'

Curtis slid off the desk and stuck his dead pipe in his mouth. 'If you say so,' he remarked stiffly. 'I just hope you have no intention of getting involved with him. That kind of man . . .'

She laughed aloud. 'Involved with him? Believe me, Curtis, that's the furthest thing from my mind. Or his.'

'Listen, Claire, if you need any more time off to rest, I'm sure it could be arranged.'

'No, thanks, Curtis. I'd just as soon keep busy.'

'Well, in that case, do you suppose you could give

some thought to this other problem Donovan saddled us with?'

'You mean the tutoring for Scott Cunningham?' she said slowly.

He nodded. 'We've only got two weeks.'

'Two weeks?' she cried. 'It would take two *years* to drill anything into that thick head.'

He spread his hands and shrugged. 'What can I say? There's an important game coming up a week from next Saturday—homecoming, you know, the razzle dazzle, the dance, the high point of the year for the whole graduates' association. Apparently, if Scott doesn't play, Rainier doesn't stand a chance of winning, and I'm told that's of crucial import to several very heavy financial supporters of the college.'

Claire got up from her desk and started pacing around the tiny room. 'I don't see how I can do anything with him in that short a time, Curtis. It's just not possible.'

'Listen, Claire,' he said on a sterner note, 'you've got to get the idea out of your head that you're going to actually *teach* the numskull anything. All you've got to do is drum enough information into him so he can feed it back to you in a test.'

She fixed him with a cold stare. 'I don't quite understand, Curtis,' she said evenly. 'I thought teaching was our job.'

'Oh, Claire, grow up,' he said testily. 'You don't have to understand. Just do it.'

When she saw the pinched look on his face and heard the unaccustomed note of severity in his voice, it suddenly occurred to her that he was terrified. Of what? Losing his job? He had tenure. They couldn't fire him. But they could block his promotion, and she knew for a fact that he coveted the job of Dean when old Professor Tewson retired next year.

'All right, Curtis,' she said quietly. 'I'll take care of it.'

Claire arranged to meet Scott that afternoon in her office. This time, she was glad to see, the burly athlete was not quite so arrogant or impertinent. He, too, seemed frightened, and definitely humbled. Even though she had been forced into this position, she was still the one who would grade his paper. That put him in her power, and he knew it.

'Now, Scott,' she said briskly, 'we're going to have to set up a schedule of tutoring sessions for you. When would be a convenient time? How about now, and say around three o'clock every afternoon here in my office?'

The boy's eyes widened. 'Oh, I can't do that, Miss Talbot. With the big game coming up in two weeks, we have practice every afternoon, and Coach Donovan will murder me if I miss a day. He only let me off today because it's so important for me to pass this course.'

She sighed deeply. 'Well, then, we'll just have to do it in the evenings. Will that suit you and your coach?'

His face brightened. 'That sounds great.'

'All right.' She thought for a minute. 'The building is locked at night, so we'll have to meet at my place. We'd better start tonight. Can you make it by eight o'clock?'

He nodded, then stumbled clumsily to his feet and stood there, his great bulk looming over her, while she wrote down her address for him. He's like a big awkward baby, she thought as she handed him the piece of paper and she wondered how on earth he managed to handle himself in an athletic contest, which surely took some grace and agility.

'I'll see you tonight, then,' she said, and turned back to the quiz she was preparing for tomorrow's class.

When she realised he was still standing there, she looked up enquiringly at him, and was startled to see that his fair complexion had gone up in flame. His head hanging down and he was folding and unfolding the piece of paper with her address on it.

Finally he met her eyes. 'Er—Miss Talbot,' he stammered. 'I—er—figure I owe you an apology for making you do this. And also for being such a dunce in your class.'

The bright blue eyes were so clear and guileless that Claire softened in spite of herself. 'Oh, that's all right, Scott. I understand.'

'But the thing is,' he went on eagerly, 'I really love football. And I'm good at it, too. Coach says he wouldn't be surprised if I got an offer from a professional team when I graduate.' His face fell. 'If I graduate, that is,' he added miserably.

'Well, I can't promise anything, Scott, but if you're willing to work hard, I see no reason why you can't do it.'

'Oh, I will.' He grinned. 'I've got to. Coach says the same thing, that it's up to me, and if you've ever seen him really mad, you know he means business.'

'I can imagine,' she retorted drily.

The blond giant shambled out the door with a wave of one enormous paw, and she went back to her work.

Every night for the next week, Claire met Scott as planned at her apartment. He was always prompt, and the sessions were long, lasting sometimes almost until midnight.

As the days passed and she came to know the boy better, her original opinion of him gradually altered. He was no mental giant, and she still had reservations about his ability to pass a legitimate test, but she found his eagerness to please her and his determination to succeed very impressive, even endearing.

Much of that eagerness, of course, was sparked by his terror of his coach and she could well imagine the high-handed, dictatorial way that autocrat ruled over his team. He didn't know the meaning of the word compromise. It would either be his way or none at all.

By the second week of the tutorial session, Claire even began to hope there was a slim chance Scott might actually pass a real test, and when Curtis checked in with her the following Monday afternoon she told him so.

'Good work, Claire,' he said with feeling. 'That would solve everything, wouldn't it?' He shook his head admiringly. 'I've got to hand it to you. I never dreamed the dunderhead could memorise the alphabet, much less the 'Prologue' to the *Canterbury Tales*.'

'He's not such a dunderhead as all that,' Claire protested. 'He's just been so wrapped up in that stupid game that he never gave himself a chance at academic pursuits. In his way, he's rather bright, in fact. He just needed a push.'

'If you say so,' Curtis remarked drily. 'At least I take it he's been good about getting to the sessions.'

'He hasn't missed one, and that's saying a lot, considering the demands that coach of his makes on his time. He runs the poor kid ragged.' She glanced at her watch. 'In fact, Scott is due here any minute.'

'I thought you were only meeting at night.'

'It was his idea to get in an extra session or two this week. You really do have to give him credit, Curtis.'

Curtis pursed his lips and narrowed his eyes at her. 'Are you sure there isn't more to it than a zeal for learning?'

'What on earth do you mean?'

'Only that perhaps he has a more personal interest in you than just as his teacher.'

She laughed aloud. 'Are you kidding? He's only a boy.'

'He's twenty-two. I looked it up. And you're twenty-four. Figure it out for yourself.'

'Believe me, Curtis, all he wants to do is pass the course, and he looks on me as his only hope. That's all there is to it.'

Still, after Curtis had gone, she had to wonder if there might not be a grain of truth in what he said. She'd been noticing a few odd things lately: several deep sighs, a tendency to move his chair closer to hers when their heads were bent together over a difficult passage. And a few times, when she was coaching him on a particularly knotty point, he'd given her some rather strange looks, looks that could only be described as calf-eyed.

No, she thought, that's silly. He only sees me as his tutor.

Just then there was a knock on her door, and Scott came inside. With a furtive glance over his shoulder, he shut the door quickly behind him, and came to sit on the chair beside her desk.

She gave him a suspicious look. 'Scott, is something wrong?'

No. Nothing's wrong.' He took a slim textbook out of his satchel. 'Can we get right at the Keats? I can't stay long.'

They worked steadily for the next hour, and once again she was encouraged by his progress. He actually seemed to understand some of the poems on his first try, without her prompting.

She was so pleased that when they'd finished she reached out a hand impulsively and laid it on his arm. 'Scott, I'm delighted with how you well you're doing. I think you'll be ready for the exam by Thursday or Friday.'

He turned beet-red and stared hard down at the floor, not saying a word, just breathing heavily. After a few seconds, he raised his head and gazed directly into her eyes. Then, to her astonishment, he suddenly grasped the hand on his arm, leaned forward and put his face close to hers.

'Miss Talbot,' he choked out. 'Claire. I can't stand

it any more. I've got to tell you how I feel about you.'

To her utter horror, he slid out of his chair and got down on his knees before her, still clutching her hand in his. Before she could get out a word or pull her hand away, he had raised it to his lips and was covering it with wet, fervent kisses.

Just then the door flew open and a wild-eyed Jake Donovan burst into the room. He took one look at the little tableau spread out before him, then marched over to Scott, who was still kneeling at her feet, and grabbed him by the scruff of the neck.

'I thought I might find you here,' he shouted. 'Just what the hell is going on?'

CHAPTER FOUR

WHILE Scott scrambled clumsily to his feet, Claire tried to think of something to say. She was so stunned by Scott's declaration of love that her head was still reeling. She stared blankly up at Jake, who was literally beside himself with fury. Having dealt with the shame-faced, incoherent Scott, he now turned his wrath on her.

'I thought the arrangement was to teach him something, not seduce him,' he ground out in a cold, menacing tone.

By then Scott had found his voice and was now charging in to defend her. 'Listen, coach,' he said in a wobbly voice, 'you have no right to blame Claire. She didn't do anything wrong.'

Jake swivelled around and fixed him with a killing look. 'Claire?' Scott shuffled his feet around noisily, and Jake poked a finger at the boy's massive chest. 'You're supposed to be at practice this afternoon. What are you doing here? Do you want to play football or not?'

'Well, yeah, sure I do, but . . .'

'Then get down to the practice field where you belong,'

Scott gave Claire a helpless look, then turned back to Jake. 'It's not her fault, coach.'

Claire spoke up then. 'Scott,' she said quietly, 'just do as he says.'

Jake stood with his arms folded across his chest, staring silently off into space until Scott had stumbled out of the room, shutting the door quietly behind him. Then he lifted his head and fixed her with a poisonous look. He opened his mouth to say something, but she beat him to it.

'Why is it so terrible for him to want to learn something?' she asked in a calm, rational tone.

'That isn't the point. He's made a commitment to the rest of the team, and I expect him to honour it. Is that so unreasonable?'

'Don't you think you might be pushing him a little too hard?'

'No, he snapped. 'I don't. And I don't need you to tell me how to handle my players.'

She could see it was hopeless. 'All right. You did what you came here to do and got what you wanted. Now, will you please go?'

'Gladly,' he said, making for the door, but before leaving he turned around to face her again. 'Just remember, teacher, your job is to see that Scott passes the test. Nothing more. What he does after Saturday's game is his own business, but until then he's going to follow my orders and quit mooning around you.'

Claire folded her arms in front of her and gave him her haughtiest look. She would have cut out her tongue before giving him the satisfaction of uttering one word in her own defence.

Their eyes locked together in a silent contest of wills that seemed to go on forever. Finally, Jake dropped his gaze to sweep her up and down in an insolent appraisal.

'Although I probably should warn him that he's only wasting his time trying to thaw out a block of ice like you, anyway.'

On Thursday, Scott took his re-sit examination, and, although Claire stuck to her guns by not making it to easy for him, she could tell that he'd done all right on his own as she started correcting it that night. His grade wouldn't be brilliant. In fact, it was barely average work. But he would pass the course, and on his own merits, without special treatment.

After the awful scene in her offfice on Monday afternoon when Jake had barged in to find Scott on his knees before her, Claire had had serious doubts that he would even show up for that evening's tutoring session. But he had arrived promptly at eight o'clock, and the subject had not been mentioned until he was leaving her apartment on Wednesday night, their last meeting.

He had hesitated at the door, then said, 'I hope you'll come to the game on Saturday. And to the dance that night.'

'Oh, I don't think so, Scott,' she'd said. 'I'm not really a football fan, and it's so long since I've danced that I've forgotten how.'

'I'd really like you to come,' he persisted.

'We'll see,' she said with a smile.

Late on Thursday night, Curtis called her at home, his voice breathless with anticipation. 'Well? Did he pass?'

'Yes, Curtis, he passed. Just barely, but he did pass. Now, as you say, everyone is happy.'

'Good work, Claire. I'll call Donovan right away and give him the good news. Or would you like to do the honours yourself? You've certainly earned it.'

'No, thanks,' she replied hastily. 'You do it.'

She hadn't forgotten the parting shot he'd levelled at her Monday afternoon, and was still smarting at its implications. He thought she was a block of ice. Was it true? And what did she care what he thought? His behaviour had been brutal that day, both to her and to Scott, and she'd never forgive him for that.

The telephone rang again the minute she and Curtis hung up. It was Kate—tonight's Thursday dinner had been cancelled and they hadn't spoken for a couple of days.

'Well?' she said with no preamble. 'Did your football player pass his test?'

'As a matter of fact, he did. I just finished grading it.'

'Thank goodness that's over. Listen, I really called to ask if you and Curtis are going to the homecoming dance on Saturday night after the game.'

'Oh, I don't think so. At least, Curtis hasn't said anything about it. He doesn't care for those affairs any more than I do.'

'Well, come with us, then. You are going to the game, aren't you?'

'I hadn't planned on it.'

'Won't your sportsman be disappointed if you don't show up?'

'I don't know. I hadn't thought about it.'

'Well, I think you should at least put in an appearance, at both the game and the dance.'

'It's fancy dress this year, isn't it?' Claire asked. 'I don't have anything to wear.'

'Oh, we can fix that. Come on. Be a sport.'

'I'll think about it and let you know,' she said, and they hung up.

Well, why shouldn't she go? She'd been to a few football games before, and always found them intensely boring. She had a personal stake in his one, however, considering her work with Scott. And he wanted her to be there.

She toyed briefly with the idea of calling Curtis to see if he planned to go, either to the game or the dance. But by now she was a little fed up with Curtis and his self-protective manoeuvring. For all his loud talk about his high ideals and academic freedom, he'd give in to pressure over Scott's grade at the first puff of wind.

She'd go, she decided at last, but without Curtis.

The day of the game was perfect football weather, clear and crisp, with the smell of woodsmoke in the air. A light frost had nipped the huge maples that lined College Avenue into brilliant shades of orange, red and gold, and a thin November sun shone directly overhead against a bright blue sky. For the past week Claire had listened to the school band practising in the stadium from her office, and even she was beginning to get into the spirit of the thing.

Kate and Harold stopped by her apartment at one o'clock that afternoon to pick her up, and they walked the five blocks to the stadium along with the crowds of others spectators, all dressed warmly against the chill wind that blew off Puget Sound, and ruddy-cheeked with excitement and cold.

Since this was to be a local game, played between two Seattle teams, there was a huge turnout, and when they climbed up the long, curving concrete ramp to their seats, the large, oval outdoor arena was already three-quarters full.

The marching band was on the grassy field, pacing through its intricate pre-game formations and loudly blaring the college song, while across the way the Rainier student section was waving colourful purple and gold banners to signal their undying support for the home team.

In spite of herself, Claire felt a little thrill of excitement at the crowds, the noise, the music, the colour. When they got to their seats, Harold moved as far away from the two women as possible on the narrow bench, dissociating himself from them so he could concentrate on the game.

By two o'clock, the band had marched off and were seated in the stands on the opposite side. Suddenly a huge yell went up as the gold-helmeted first-string Rainier team came charging out through the tunnel on to the playing field, with their coach running along at their head.

'Donovan, Donovan,' the crowd started chanting, and the tall man gave them a brief wave on his way to the bench.

Then the two teams lined up facing each other at the fifty-yard line, a whistle was blown, the ball was snapped and kicked high in the air, and the game was under way.

'Now,' Kate yelled in her ear above the roar, 'aren't you glad you came?'

'Yes,' Claire shouted back. 'I only wish I understood what was going on.'

'You don't have to,' Kate replied cheerfully. 'All you need to know right now is that Rainier won the toss, which means your friend Scott is the one carrying the ball. He's number forty. Just keep your eyes on him.'

Five minutes into the game, Claire was so confused that she couldn't even tell the team apart, much less keep track of number forty. During the brief intervals where she did manage to keep her eye on Scott in the scramble of players, she was amazed at the grace and precision of his movements, and would hardly have recognised the awkward hulk who could barely manage to leave a room without stumbling over his own feet.

Throughout most of the game Jake stood with his arms folded across his chest, watching every move on the field. Occasionally he would shout an order at his players on the field or pace up and down the sidelines in front of the bench, but for the most part he was grimly still and silent.

When the final shot was fired, signalling the end of the game, the Rainier student section went wild, pouring down on to the field *en masse*, tearing down the goal-posts and clustering around their triumphant gladiators. Then, as one man, the weary, bedraggled players hoisted their coach up on their shoulders and carried him around to the exit tunnel.

Kate was jubilant. 'We did it!' she shouted. 'We won!'

'So I gathered,' Claire remarked.

'And Scott is the hero of the game,' Kate went on excitedly. 'You'll have to give Jake Donovan credit, Claire. He's certainly worked miracles with the team, and you can bet he'll be the man of the hour around here for some time.'

That night, when Claire walked into the gymnasium where the dance was being held, Kate's words were still ringing in her ears. The name of Jake Donovan seemed to be on everyone's lips. Man of the hour, indeed! she thought. If they only knew what a selfish, even ruthless man he really was, they wouldn't think he was such a paragon.

Although it was a costume ball, it was not a masquerade. Since no one wore a mask, Claire recognised several familiar faces as she made her way into the crowd, literally pushed ahead by Kate, and it wasn't long before she began to grow intensely uncomfortable under the frankly startled stares received from the people who greeted her.

She'd argued with Kate about the costume she'd devised for her, even threatening not to go to the dance at all if she had to wear it, but Kate, persistent as always, had won in the end. She had decided that Claire had the perfect figure and colouring for a Greek goddess, and had put together a diaphanous cloud of gauzy material held up by thin straps that came down to cross under her full breast and girdle her slim waist.

It hadn't seemed quite so bad when she was at home in front of her own mirror. In fact, she'd been rather pleased at her totally altered appearance, which turned out to be really rather glamorous. Kate had helped her with a subdued make-up job and arranged her thick auburn hair so that it was bound up in a loose twist at the top of her head, the ends streaming loose down her back, with little curling tendrils in front of her ears.

Now, however, among her co-workers, with the music playing loudly in the background, she felt absolutely naked, and it wasn't long before she started looking for something to hide behind. Kate, however, resplendent as Scarlett O'Hara, was having none of that, and insisted on dragging her bodily along with her wherever she went.

She caught sight of Scott right away, his enormous bulk towering over everyone else in the room. He was dressed as a Viking, wearing a brief leather skirt, his hugely muscled chest bare, and carrying a spear. He had sandals on his feet, with thongs wrapped around his sturdy legs up to the knee.

He was surrounded by a bevy of beauties dressed in the skimpiest possible costumes, but the minute he laid eyes on Claire he brushed off their clinging hands and began to make his way towards her through the crowd. The closer he came, the wider his stare grew, until he stood before her with eyes half goggling out of his head.

'You look . . .' he stammered, staring down at her. 'You look so different,' he finally got out.

'Congratulations, Scott,' she said with a smile. 'I hear you're the hero of the day.'

'Were you there?' he asked eagerly. 'Did you see me play?'

She nodded. 'I was very impressed, too. I didn't understand much of what was going on, but I did manage to keep my eye on you most of the time.'

He grinned. 'That's good.'

The school orchestra had been playing dance tunes, but now all of a sudden it stopped. There was a ringing noise in the PA system, and all eyes turned towards the bandstand, where the president of the college was now calling for their attention.

'I'll make this brief,' he said into the microphone, evoking a cheer of approval from the crowd. He cleared his throat and went on. 'But I think we all want to show our appreciation for the great job done today by our football coach.' Another louder cheer. 'And so, without further ado, I'd like to introduce the man of the hour, Jake Donovan!' His eyes searched the room, then he becokoned with his hand. 'Come on up here, Jake, and say a few words.'

As the crowd broke into loud applause, Claire craned her neck to see him, but it wasn't until he finally—and obviously reluctantly—made his way up the steps that she got her first look at him.

He strode over to the microphone, then paused, his arms hanging loosely at his sides, while the crowd broke into a loud cheer, clapping, whistling, stamping their feet. He was dressed as a pirate, and had on tight black breeches, flowing white shirt unbuttoned to the waist and a patch over one eye. He looked every inch and stood there now with his hands on his lean hips, his long legs slightly apart, waiting for the crowd to settle down.

When it was finally quiet, he began to speak in a low, well-modulated and totally self-assured tone of voice. 'Thank you,' he said. 'It was a great day for all of us here at Rainier College, but I have to tell you that the real credit goes to the team. I ran them hard this season, and besides all the hours of practice they had to put in, they all had to keep up their academic programme as well. You can be proud of them, as I am, for the discipline and dedication shown by each and every one. Thank you again.'

With that, he gave the crowd a brief wave and jumped lightly down from the stage, to further cheers. The band began to play then, and soon a few couples drifted out on to the dance-floor.

Scott, still standing at Claire's side, turned to her. 'Will you dance with me?'

From then on, everything happened so fast that Claire became swept along mindlessly on a heady wave of sheer excitement. After that first flush of embarrassment at the reaction of her friends to her scanty costume, her self-consciousness gradually dissipated as she danced every dance.

Although one after another of the men she worked with asked her to dance, some of whom she hardly knew, Scott was never far from her side, and it seemed she always ended up with him sooner or later. Once in a while she caught sight of the tall, dark pirate, always with some beauty hanging on him, but she was having such a good time herself that she didn't give him much thought.

Curtis showed up eventually, dressed as a French dancer, with a striped shirt, and a red band tied around his head. The moment he laid eyes on her, he came rushing over to claim a dance from her.

'I hardly recognised you, Claire,' he remarked as he waltzed her away sedately under Scott's crestfallen gaze. 'You look like an entirely different person.'

Although his tone was appreciative, Claire detected an underlying note of criticism in his words, and she could feel her spirits sagging as shades of her original self-doubt and unease began to return in full force.

'It sounds as though you don't quite approve,' she remarked lightly.

He stepped back, holding her loosely at arm's length, and shrugged. 'Well, you'll have to admit it's not quite the proper image for a young teacher to project around her students. I couldn't help noticing, for example, that the Cunningham boy could hardly take his eyes off you. Or his hands.'

That was going a little too far, and Claire felt a prick of annoyance at his high-handed, pedantic tone. 'Well, as you yourself pointed out, he's hardly a boy,' she rejoined tartly.

Curtis pursed his lips and frowned. 'And just what is that supposed to mean? Surely you're not thinking of . . .'

'Oh, come on, Curtis,' she broke in. 'Why don't you try to loosen up a little? After all, we're here to celebrate and have a good time.'

'Claire, there is such a thing as propriety, you know,' he said solemnly. 'It's one thing to celebrate, but quite another to make a public spectacle of yourself.'

She stopped short in the middle of the floor and drew back from him, really irritated by now. For the first time since she'd known him, she saw what a petty little man he really was. She had just about made up her mind to tell him what she thought of his small-minded attitude when she suddenly felt a hand come around her waist from behind and heard Jake Donovan's firm, deep voice.

'May I?' he asked smoothly, and before either she or Curtis could utter a word he had turned her around to face him and was dancing her away with long, confident strides. As soon as they were out of earshot, he looked down at her and said in an amused tone, 'Having a little trouble there with the boyfriend?'

At the teasing tone, all the past trouble she'd had with this man came back to her. She stiffened and tried to pull away from him, but he only tightened his hold on her.

'He's not my boyfriend,' she said through her teeth, and was immediately sorry when she saw the grin of satisfaction spread slowly on his face.

'That's good,' he said, and pulled her even closer.

He didn't say anything more, just hummed, a little off-key, under his breath, and kept propelling her masterfully across the dance-floor. He was so much taller than Curtis, his legs so much longer and his hold on her so much tighter that all she could do was allow herself to be carried away.

As they danced, she had to wonder just what was going on here. The last time they'd met, he'd acted more as though he'd like to strangle her than dance with her. The answer seemed clear enough. Although he obviously had his pick of desirable women, a man with his vanity would have to make a conquest of all of them, including one he didn't even like much.

For some reason, though, it didn't seem to matter, and even that dubious honour did a lot for her ego, especially after the bruising encounter with Curtis. Besides, the celebratory mood and the heady sensation of being sought after tonight by several men who'd never even noticed her before made her a little reckless.

She'd come back to earth with a bang soon enough when it was over, and she could always fend him off later if he got amorous again. She'd done it once before, after all. Deciding that she might as well relax and enjoy it while it lasted, she closed her eyes and allowed her body to melt against his.

After a while, it seemed that the music was growing fainter, and she felt a definite chill on her bare shoulders. She opened her eyes to see that he had danced her out into the covered portico at the side of the gym.

'Are you cold?' he asked in a low voice.

'Yes, a little.'

'Let's go to my office. It's warm in there.'

She eyed him suspiciously. 'What for?'

'I want to talk to you.'

'What about?'

He frowned. 'You have a very suspicious nature, Professor. I'm not going to attack you. I just want to talk.' He paused. 'I've been thinking a lot about what's happened between us, and I might owe you an apology.'

'All right. That's fair enough. Apology accepted. What's there to talk about?'

He gave her a hurt look. 'Well, there's a little more to it than that. I was hoping we could be friends.'

His hands were on her bare arms now, holding her loosely. She shivered again. It would be the height of folly to allow this man to persuade her to go alone with him to his office. And what did he mean by his statement that he wanted to be friends? She looked up at him, trying to fathom what he had on his mind. She couldn't trust him an inch, she knew that, but she was so curious by now that she felt compelled to find out.

'All right,' she said at last. 'But just for a few minutes.'

He put an arm lightly around her shoulders and they walked together down towards the back of the building. The sky was still clear, with millions of stars twinkling overhead and an enormous yellow harvest moon hanging in the dark blue sky.

After they'd gone about thirty feet, he stopped and took a bunch of keys out of his pocket. She watched him as he bent to unlock the door. The moonlight cast a bright gleam on to his smooth dark hair and cast interesting shadows on his lean face. The pirate costume suited him perfectly, the long, full sleeves billowing down from his broad shoulders, the tight black breeches hugging his slim hips.

He pushed the door open, stepped back a pace and motioned her inside. There was one small lamp burning on a very neat desk in the centre of the room. Somehow she had expected a lot of clutter, that it would be filled with athletic equipment and the pungent odour of a men's locker-room. Instead, it looked more like the rather elegant private office of a busy corporate executive.

There were hunting prints on the walls, a few photographs of sports figures in action, a filing cabinet in one corner of the room and against the opposite wall a low leather couch. A faint odour of tobacco and a mild, pleasant soap hung in the air and, as he had promised, it was blessedly warm.

He closed the door and leaned back against it, his arms folded across his chest, eyeing her carefully. 'You look surprised,' he remarked casually. 'What were you expecting? A den of iniquity with nude pin-ups on the wall?'

She had to smile. 'No, not really.' She walked over to a group of photographs over the couch and inspected them. 'But I am impressed by how neat you are.'

He came to stand a little behind her. 'Ah, that's my organisational skill.'

'It's an impressive office,' she said. 'At least as large and comfortable as the president's.'

'That was part of the bargain when I agreed to come here: an office I could use to conduct my business affairs.'

She turned her head and looked up at him. 'That's right. I heard that you don't receive a salary. What is your other business? Or is that prying?'

'Not at all. I still have some dealings with athletic

supply companies, old endorsement contracts from the days when my name meant something in the world of professional football. A few investments, nothing spectacular. I like to dabble in the stock market.'

'You were a business major, weren't you?'

'That right. Fascinating stuff, the economy.'

She laughed. 'It's all Greek to me, I'm afraid.'

He crossed over to a beautiful carved mahogany cupboard in the corner. 'Would you like a drink? It'll warm you up.'

'Yes,' she said after a moment's hesitation. 'I guess so.'

'Sit down, then, and I'll fix us a brandy and soda. No ice I'm afraid. Is that OK?

'That's fine.'

She sat down gingerly on the edge of the couch, hugging her arms and watching him as he made the drinks. Somehow her costume seemed even scantier now that she was alone in here with this man, and even though it was quite warm inside, she was still shivering. Yet she suspected it was from nerves by now more than the cold.

He came back and handed her a glass, then sat down beside her, some distance away. 'Cheers,' he said, raising his glass.

She took one sip of the drink, then another. As the brandy slid down her throat, it did seem to warm her a little, but she was still jumpy. She looked over at him. He was leaning forward with his elbows on his knees, his long legs spread apart, holding his drink in his hands between them.

'You said you wanted to talk to me,' she said.

'Yes.' He leaned back against the arm of the couch. 'Now that it's all over—Scott's academic problems, the big game—I've had a little time to think over the way I've behaved to you, and I don't like it much.' He raised a hand and rubbed the back of his neck. 'I want you to know that I understand how you would think an education is far more important than a stupid game. I guess I still get too carried away with it. I should have tried harder to see your point of view.'

Nothing he could have said would have surprised her more.

'Well, I wasn't exactly a paragon of tact and understanding myself,' she said slowly. 'And it's really not much a stupid game. I admit I don't know what's going on most of the time, but I quite enjoy the excitement and the spectacle. And as you say, it's all over now anyway.'

'Well, that's just it,' he said with a quirky smile. 'That's what I wanted to talk to you about. I don't want it to end.'

'What do you mean? You don't want what to end?'

He tilted his head back, downing his drink, and she watched, mesmerised, at the working of his long throat as he swallowed. The loose pirate shirt revealed a large expanse of smooth, tanned chest, more heavily muscled than she would have guessed from his slim, lithe appearance in ordinary clothes.

Then he looked directly into her eyes. 'You and me,' he said briefly.

'I still don't understand. Are you saying . . .'

'I'm saying exactly what it sounds like. I want to

get to know you better, see more of you.'

'Why?'

His eyes flew open. 'Why? Well, for the same reason any man wants to get to know a woman.' He shrugged. 'To have a good time, to do things together, to find out if there's any chemistry between us.' He slid his body closer and gave her a broad grin. 'Although I think we both already know the answer to that.'

'You certainly do come right to the point,' she remarked.

'I've found it saves a lot of time.'

'I'll just bet you have,' she murmured, almost inaudibly.

His suggestion had thrown her into total confusion. Men like Jake Donovan just didn't say things like that to her, and she didn't know how to respond, or even how she should react. On the one hand, it could be considered an insult that he saw her as one more easy conquest, but, on the other, it was quite flattering that he would even bother.

In any event, she didn't see that she had anything to lose by playing along with him for a while just to see what his intentions were. She was sick of her dead-end relationship with Curtis, and had lost all respect for him over this affair with Scott. And as for Scott, although she was flattered by his interest in her, she looked upon him as an immature child, in spite of their closeness in age. Jake Donovan, on the other hand, was a real man.

In the meantime, he had moved even closer, so that their bodies were touching now. She held her breath, watching, as one hand reached out slowly to touch her bare shoulder. As his long fingers tightened, a pleasant warmth began to travel all the way up and down her arm until it filled her whole body.

A strange, tingling sensation was coursing through her very bloodstream now, arousing in her at the same time a definite desire for more and just a touch of apprehension. What would he expect from her? She began to shiver again.

'You're still cold,' he murmured at her ear.

Before she could deny it, his arm had snaked around her, and he had lowered his head to place his lips against her shoulder. She drew in a sharp breath and held herself utterly still, unable to speak or move. His mouth was at the side of her neck now, nuzzling under her jaw. His arms tightened, and she turned wordlessly to face him.

In the dim light cast by the lamp on the desk he looked so beautiful. The green eyes glowed with desire, and the shadows made the bony planes of his cheeks and jaw stand out in sharp relief. Unable to stop herself, she closed her eyes and allowed her body to sink against his.

CHAPTER FIVE

WHEN Jake's seeking mouth found hers at last, it was like coming home after a long absence, or finding a safe harbour after years of searching. The kiss began with a gentle exploration, his mouth brushing lightly over hers. Gradually, as the pressure increased and became more insistent, Claire simply gave herself up to it.

After a time he drew back, and when she opened her eyes he was gazing down at her, his eyes glowing with frank desire. The dark hair was falling over his forehead, and his chest was heaving, his breath coming in short rasps. Then, without a word, his mouth opened, and came down on hers with such punishing pressure that she was forced back on the couch and he was lying half on top of her.

His hot tongue probed past her lips, parting them, until finally, with a sigh, she gave up her resistance and opened herself to him. The hand on her shoulder moved down now, sliding over the gauzy material of her costume until it covered her breast. Then she felt it slip under the loose bodice on to her hot, bare skin, his long fingers playing about the hardened nipple, and setting up such a painful ache that she moaned aloud.

She could feel the hardness of his lower body

pressing against her thigh, and knew he was as aroused as she was. He began to tug at the bodice of her dress now, pulling the straps down over her shoulder so that her breast was exposed. Startled, she tried to raise her head, but, when his mouth left hers and bent lower to take the throbbing peak into his mouth, she could only sink back with a sigh and give herself up completely to the ecstasy of the moment.

Then, as his lips worked their magic on her breast, his other hand began to travel downwards, over her ribcage, her waist, her stomach, until it finally moved purposefully over her thighs. It was then that the nagging apprehension at the back of her mind finally made itself clearly heard.

This time she struggled in earnest, so that he couldn't ignore it. The mouth at her breast moved up over her neck and chin, seeking hers, but she twisted her head to one side, and reached down to cover herself. He raised his head and stared down at her, a puzzled frown on his face.

'What's wrong?' he whispered harshly. 'Did I hurt you?'

Oh, God, she thought, he's going to accuse me of being a tease again. 'Jake,' she said shakily, 'you're moving way too fast for me. You—you frighten me.'

He looked away and stared thoughtfully into space. When he finally turned back to her, he reached down to slide the straps of her dress back into position on her shoulder and pulled her up beside him.

'You're right,' he said. 'I'm sorry. I guess I got carried away. I should have realised . . .' He broke off and smiled crookedly. 'It's just that you do weird things to my libido, teacher.'

He rose to his feet, and reached down a hand to help her up. Then he put his arms around her and held her in a loose embrace. After a moment, he put his hands on her shoulders, kneading them gently, and looked down into her eyes.

'Are you OK?'

She nodded. 'Yes. Jake, I hope you don't think I was just—you know, what you said before.'

He shook his head solemnly. 'I don't think anything, except that I like you, I want to get to know you better, and I only hope I haven't blown it by moving too fast.'

'No,' she murmured with relief. 'You haven't blown it.'

Actually, she found his fervour immensely flattering. She'd never known a man to lose control of himself over her before, and it was quite a heady experience.

'Good. Then shall we try again? We can have dinner one night next week and take it in slower stages. How does that sound?'

It sounded heavenly to her, but she didn't want to appear as eager to him as she felt. 'Yes. I'd like that.'

'Do you want to go back to the dance now? Or I can take you home if you'd rather.'

'No,' she said quickly. 'I don't think so. I came with friends, and I think it would be best if I went home with them. They're probably looking for me right now.'

'Not that wimpy Gregg character, I hope,' he said severely. 'Or Scott.'

Her first impulse was to rush in with an explanation that neither man meant a thing to her, but then she decided he didn't need that kind of reassurance, and it wouldn't do to appear *that* easy to get.

'No,' she said. 'Not tonight.'

They went outside, and after Jake had locked the door to his office they started walking slowly down towards the ballroom. As they came closer, the dance music and the noise of the crowd grew louder and louder, shifting Claire suddenly back into the world of reality. At the entrance she saw Kate and Harold, their coats on, obviously ready to leave, and her heart sank.

The last thing she wanted right now was for Kate to find out there was anything at all going on between them. It was still too uncertain. She'd never dealt with a man like Jake Donovan before, and she was totally unsure of herself.

For all she knew, he was only being polite, and she'd never hear from him again after tonight. It would be too humiliating to have the whole world know she was attracted to him if that were to happen.

'There you are,' Kate called, and started walking briskly towards them. 'I've been looking all over for you.'

Then, as they moved into the bright glow coming from the dance-floor, Kate stopped short. She just stood there, speechless for once in her life.

'I'm sorry, Kate,' Claire said. 'Jake wanted to show me his office. Are you ready to leave?'

'Well, yes, I guess so,' Kate hedged. 'But there's no need for you to . . .'

'No,' Claire said, forestalling the offer to let her go home with Jake that she knew was coming. 'I'm ready to go if you are.'

Kate gave her a sharp, enquiring look, but Claire deliberately kept her eyes averted. 'Do you and Harold know Jake?' she asked. She turned to the man at her side. 'Jake, these are my good friends, Kate and Harold Dawson.'

While the two men shook hands, Kate kept staring at her, trying to catch her eye, but Claire managed to avoid it. She'd hear what was on her friend's mind soon enough on the way home, and she steeled herself for the barrage of questions she knew lay ahead.

The introductions over, the two men started to discuss the day's game, but Claire interrupted them. 'Goodnight, then, Jake. And congratulations again on your success today.'

Jake nodded politely. 'Goodnight.' He hesitated a moment, as though sensing her anxiety to get away, then added in a low voice, 'I'll call you later in the week.'

'All right,' she said.

She took Kate firmly by the arm and steered her in the direction of the car park. It was freezing cold after the warmth of Jake's cosy office, and she was anxious to get home as soon as possible. She had a lot of thinking to do, and wanted to do it in peace.

As he feared, the moment they were out of earshot Kate started on her. 'Well, what was that all about?' she hissed in Claire's ear.

'Kate, do we have to talk about it tonight?'

'Well, no, of course not, not if you don't want to,'

Kate replied huffily. 'I was just a little curious to know why you vanished like that with a man you claimed you detested just a few days ago. And what's this about him calling you? What exactly happened in that office of his?'

The steady stream of probing questions kept up all the way to the car and continued for the entire ride home. Most of them Claire fended off as deftly as possible without actually hurting her friend's feelings, but mainly she only grunted non-committally and let Kate ramble on.

Having arrived at last in front of her building, she quickly got out of the car and leaned down at the open window.

'Thanks very much for the ride. And for talking me me into going. I had a wonderful time.'

Then, before Kate could get a word out, she turned and ran up the steps. When she'd unlocked the door, she turned to wave, and watched them drive away with a sigh of relief.

Inside her own apartment, she switched on the lights, then went over to the hall mirror. She stood there for several moments, gazing thoughtfully at her reflection, as though searching for some drastic change in her appearance. She closed her eyes, remembering.

But now that she was alone, away from his warmth, the magic of his hands and mouth, his very pressure, the whole episode began to seem more and more like a lovely but distant dream.

He wouldn't call her. She would be a fool to count on that. Like Cinderalla, she would soon return to reality with a dull thud. It would probably be better that way. She couldn't hope to hold the interest of a man like Jake Donovan for long, or cope with his expertise in affairs of the heart.

Passing through the living-room on her way to bed, she glanced over at the bookcase near her desk. The neat rows of colourful binding seemed like old familiar friends. She was safe with them.

But he did call her. It wasn't until the following Wednesday, however, and by then even the tiny seed of hope Claire hadn't quite been able to squelch had died.

She was in her office when the telephone rang, standing at her desk and gazing out of the window at a steady, pounding rain. When she heard Jake's voice, her heart began to thud so hard that she was certain he could hear it on the other end of the line. Dizzy with relief and sheer nerves, she sank down slowly in her chair.

'Would you like to have dinner with me on Saturday night?' His tone was casual, just as though it wasn't the most momentous question asked throughout the entire history of mankind.

She started to speak, found she couldn't, and put her hand over the receiver while she cleared her throat. 'Yes,' she managed at last. 'I'd like that.'

'Good. I thought it might be fun to play tourist, maybe take in the Space Needle. Then later we can fool around the Center. There's always something going on. How does that sound?'

'It sounds great.' She didn't add that she was

probably the only person in Seattle who had never been to the elegant revolving restaurant high atop the familiar landmark.

'I'll pick you up around seven. OK?'

'OK.'

'And Claire——'

'Yes?'

His voice was lowered to a deep husky tone. 'I don't suppose I could talk you into wearing that great dress you had on the other night at the dance.'

Her heart gave a leap, and she covered it with a shaky laugh. 'Afraid not. That was a costume, not meant for public display.'

'Too bad. You looked good enough to eat.'

When they'd hung up, Claire could hardly restrain herself from getting up and dancing around the room. She'd need a new dress, that was essential. Her wardrobe simply wouldn't bear thinking about. What was good enough for Curtis Gregg and his boring staff dinners was hardly what a man like Jake Donovan would appreciate.

By seven-thirty on Saturday night, Claire was certain he wasn't going to come. she'd been ready for an hour. Her new woollen dress fitted her to perfection, hugging her narrow waist and subtly enhancing her full breast, a muted shade of apricot that complemented her dramatic colouring without fighting with it. Not wanting to enlist Kate's help with her make-up, she had finally settled for a light dusting of powder, a clear bronze lip gloss and a touch of mascara.

After she had swept her long auburn hair into two deep waves over her ears and pinned it back in a looser coil than usual at the nape of her neck, she knew she'd done all she could, and one last quick survey in the bedroom mirror convinced her that at lest she looked her best.

By five minutes past seven she had started pacing the floor, and half an hour later she was certain he had stood her up. What she couldn't figure out was why. Why go to the trouble to call her and ask her to dinner with him, then fail to show up?

When the doorbell rang, she almost tripped over her own feet. She was a little unsteady in her new high-heeled gold sandals to begin with, and she had to make herself stop short in the middle of the room to catch her breath before letting him in. Finally, she smoothed her skirt down, then proceeded in a deliberately slow, sedate pace to the door and opened it.

He looked absolutely gorgeous in a rather formal dark blue suit, white dress shirt and striped tie. His deep, chestnut-coloured hair had been recently cut and was combed neatly. He was freshly shaven, and as he moved past her she caught a faint whiff of masculine aftershave.

'Sorry I'm late,' he said immediately. 'There's a game on at the Kingdome, and traffic was lining up right as far as the West Seattle bridge.'

It occurred to her then that she had no idea where he lived. Where were you coming from?' she asked.

'From home.'

'And where is that?'

'Oh, I guess I never told you. I have a condo in Madison Park, on the lake.'

'You must have a boat, then.'

'You bet. A sixty-foot Chris Craft. I take it up to the San Juan Islands every summer. I'll take you out for a sail when the weather gets better in the spring.'

Claire's heart sank. Totally unable to learn to swim in spite of years of childhood lessons, she was terrified of the water. But by spring he'd probably be long gone out of her life anyway.

In the three days since he had called, she had given the matter a great deal of serious thought. She might be a closet romantic, but she was not stupid, and she was well aware that a man like this would never settle for one woman at a time. She also knew herself well enough to realise that she could never tolerate sharing him. Her intention was to enjoy being with him so long as she could stay in control of the situation, then let him go when he got tired of trying to get her into bed. She was absolutely certain that, once she allowed that to happen, he would quickly lose interest in her.

She suddenly became aware that he was staring at her. 'Did you say something?' she asked. 'I'm afraid I tend to be a little absent-minded.'

'No. I didn't say anything. I was just looking.'

The frankly appreciative expression on his lean face as he gave her a sweeping head-to-foot survey sent a warm flush over her cheeks. She was both embarrassed and pleased at the same time.

'I see,' she said in a light tone. 'Do I pass?'

He took a step towards her, covering the gap between them, and lightly touched her face. 'With honours,' he murmured, and bent his head to kiss her lightly on the mouth. 'If you're ready to go,' he said, 'I made reservations for eight o'clock. We can just make it if we leave now.'

'I'll just get my coat, then,' she said, crossing over to the hall cupboard.

She took out her good black wool dress coat, but before she could put it on he had taken it out of her hands and was holding it up for her. She turned around and reached back to slip her arms inside the sleeves, and when he had settled it on her shoulders, his hands remained there for a moment, his body pressing against hers.

Claire's head started to swim. He was so close to her that she could hear his soft breath coming near her ear and smell the clean, masculine scent of his hair and skin. She closed her eyes trying hard to remember her promise to herself that she would stay in control. What her heart wanted was to remain exactly where she was forever, but her head told her something entirely different.

With a heroic effort, she took a step away from him. 'Shall we go, then?' she asked, walking towards the door.

He was right behind her, ready to open it for her, and, if he was disappointed in her abrupt withdrawal, his face didn't reveal it. On the contrary, he was smiling broadly, just as though he had caught her out in a rather childish trick.

The Space Needle was located in the Seattle Center, in the heart of the city, and, since the area was also the home of the Opera House, the Food Fair, Science Pavilion and sports arena, it was always busy. Jake parked in the covered garage on Mercer Street, and they walked the few short blocks to the tall, thin structure that dominated the city skyline.

Going up all the way to the top in the glass-enclosed lift for the first time was quite a thrill for Claire, and one she wasn't sure she wanted to repeat soon. It was a clear, cold night, and as they were borne swiftly upwards the lights of the city's tall buildings and the ships in the busy harbour were spread out in a brilliant panorama.

As though sensing her unease, Jake kept his hand firmly on her elbow during the seemingly endless ride, and when they reached the top floor he guided her out into the lobby of the restaurant.

'The first flight is the hardest,' he remarked casually as he strolled over to the reservation desk. 'Next time you won't even notice the height.'

When they were seated at a table by a window, Claire forgot her initial discomfort at being so high, and gazed with fascination at the constantly changing view. The circular restaurant rotated so slowly that there was no sensation of motion, but every five minutes or so a new part of the city was revealed.

She looked at Jake, to see him watching her with an amused twinkle in his green eyes. 'Getting seasick?' he asked.

'No, not at all. It's wonderful—now that I'm here.'

'Worried about the trip down?'

'No,' she said honestly. She thought she would never worry about another thing in the world with his reassuring presence at her side, but she could hardly tell him that.

The waitress came to their table then, handed them dinner menus and asked if they wanted drinks. Jake cast an enquiring look at Claire. 'How about it?'

'I'd like a glass of cream sherry, please.'

'Make mine a vodka gimlet,' Jake said.

When the waitress was gone, he leaned back in his chair, pulled out a packet of cigarettes and offered her one.

'No, thanks,' she said.

'He lit one for himself, and put the pack away, blowing out smoke. 'Given it up, have you, like every other sensible person?'

'I just never tried it.'

'Wise girl.'

'I'm surprised that you do, though. I thought athletes lived such pure lives.'

At that he spluttered, choking a little on his cigarette, and reached for his water. 'Sorry,' he gasped, gulping down the entire glass. 'I don't know where you heard that, but it's definitely a fabrication. It's true that when an athlete is in training he shouldn't smoke or drink or fool around, but it's been a long time since I've been active in the game. Besides, I limit myself to two or three a day. Everything in moderation, you know, and they go well with a drink before dinner.'

'Speaking of the game,' she said, 'just why did you quit playing football? Someone told me you were at the height of your powers when you left.'

'That's not quite true. I was at a point where

I'd done what I'd set out to do, competed with the best in the game and succeeded. There was nowhere to go but down. I decided not to hang around until I was forced to quit.'

'Do you miss it?'

He thought a moment, smoking, then said, 'Yes, of course. I miss the excitement, the crowds, the cheers. But I don't miss having an entire defensive team with an average weight of two hundred pounds of solid muscle catching me behind my own line and doing their best to beat me into the ground.'

She made a face. 'That sounds terrible! How in the world did you ever get into such a dangeous job?'

He shrugged and ground out his cigarette. 'I was good at it,' he said simply. 'Isn't that the reason anyone does anything? You, for instance. From what Scott tells me, you're a damned good teacher, with a remarkable ability to communicate your enthusiasm for your subject to your students. Isn't that reason enough to stick with it?'

'I suppose so,' she said slowly. 'I guess I never thought of it in quite that way. I just sort of drifted into teaching as the best way to use a subject I was drawn to, anyway.'

'See what I mean? It's the same thing.'

She laughed. 'Yes, but I don't get my bones broken in the process.'

'No, but you do have to contend with recalcitrant students, like Scott, for example. Or,' he went on, grinning, 'bullheaded coaches and graduates' associations.'

The waitress came back with their drinks then,

and they both turned to consult their menus.

It was almost midnight when they finally drove back to her apartment. After a wonderful dinner, they had strolled around the Center. There was a band concert in the arena, a drum and bugle corps marching in the coliseum, and they ended up at the Food Fair for a Beligian waffle with strawberries and a steaming cup of coffee.

The traffic was light at this time of night, and they didn't have far to go. It had been a perfect evening, by far the best Claire could ever remember, and she hated to see it end. As they neared her street, however, she began to experience a slight tremor of anxiety at what lay ahead.

The trouble was, she *liked* him. He was fun to be with, easy to talk to, and not once during the evening had there been the slightest hint of pressure on her, not even so much as a suggestive word or tone of voice. They'd simply had a very good time together. Although she was still determined that she must stay in control of the situation, she dreaded the possibility that the lovely evening would end in a contest of wills.

He pulled up at the kerb in front of her apartment, switched off the engine, and moved his arm up over the back of her seat. 'It's been a great evening, Claire,' he said.

She turned to him. 'Yes, it has. Thank you very much.' Her words sounded stilted and overly polite, just like a good little girl reciting a stock phrase of courtesy. 'I really enjoyed myself, Jake,' she added in a warmer tone.

The arm slid down to settle around her shoulders, and he reached out his other hand to place it on her cheek. 'Are you going to invite me in for a nightcap?' he said in a low, husky voice.

She was immediately thrown into a state of confusion. She had been anticipating the question all the way home and made up her mind to refuse, but when it finally came her mind just couldn't seem to function rationally. His fingers were moving lightly over her face, touching her mouth, her eyes, smoothing the deep wings of hair back behind her ears.

'I'm a little tired,' she said uncertainly, and made a feeble attempt to move an inch or so away from his disturbing presence. 'Maybe some other time.'

'OK,' he said promptly. 'I understand.'

She was so astonished at his easy acquiescence that she was totally unprepared for his next move. Instead of releasing her and backing away, as she had expected, the hand on her face was suddenly gripping the back of her neck hard, and his mouth had come down to cover hers, opening her mouth in a deep kiss.

She felt herself weakening, sinking into a passionate and instinctive response to the warmth of his mouth and tongue. Her head fell back, and she closed her eyes. There wasn't a thought in her head except that she never wanted it to end. With his strong arms around her, his mobile mouth pressed against hers, an intense heat was building up to fill her whole body, creating such a heavy lethargy in her that any movement, even any thought, seemed utterly beyond her strength.

When his hand came around to cover her breast,

however, she became instantly alert, suddenly aware that she was moving dangerously close to the point of no return. A few minutes more and he'd be inside her apartment, in spite of all her firm resolutions. She had to put a stop to it right now, while she still could.

His hand was moving slowly back and forth over her breasts now, lingering to play lightly over each taut peak, which were clearly discernible under the thin wool of her dress.

She drew in a deep breath, put her hand over his and pulled it away. There was a slight resistance, but then, as though sensing she really meant business, he wrapped his arms around her and drew her to him gently, resting his chin on the top of her head. He held her like that for a long time, motionless and silent, as though needing to get himself under control before he said anything.

Claire was perfectly content to remain just as they were. She loved the feel of his strong arms around her, his heart beating so close to her own. There was nothing to threaten her now, and gradually she allowed herself to relax against him.

Reassured by her success in taming him, at least for a moment, and without thinking what she was doing, she raised a hand and laid it on his chest, directly over his heart. She'd never really touched him before, she thought dreamily, as her palm pressed against the flat, hard muscles and planes.

Immediately he tensed, then put his hands on her shoulders and pushed her away. 'Don't do that,' he said curtly.

'I'm sorry,' she stammered. 'I was only . . .'

'Listen,' he said in a more conciliatory tone, 'I realise you haven't had a lot of experience, but you should be able to figure it out for yourself. It's one thing to turn a guy down, but quite another to make an about-face like that and start to lead him on again.'

'Jake,' she said, appalled, 'I had no idea! Please, believe me, I didn't mean to do that. Honestly.'

'I know. And *I* understand. I'm just warning you. The next guy might not be so understanding. A man can get very ugly when he's teased like that.'

'I—I don't know what to say.' She felt so ashamed. She bent her head and covered her face with her hands.

Then, gently, he pried them away. He put one finger under her chin and tilted her head up so that she was gazing directly into his eyes. The lines of his jaw were taut, and his mouth set in a firm line, but when he spoke his voice was kind.

'Claire, I think you're going to have to do some soul-searching soon. You're a real romantic at heart, who's spent most of her life with her nose buried in a book. Now, believe me, I have no quarrel with that. In fact it's one of the things that appeals to me most about you, that remote, untouched quality of yours. But it also makes me feel possessive, maybe even a little greedy. I've never known anyone like you, and I don't want this thing between us to end before it gets off the ground.'

Claire's head was spinning. 'I'm not sure I understand,' she said at last. 'What exactly are you trying to tell me?'

He reached up and ran a hand over his hair. 'I'm

not one hundred per cent sure,' he said with a wry smile. 'I just want to get the point across that we're not characters in a book here, or actors in a play. Nor are we children. This is real life, Claire. We're two adult, flesh and blood people. I guess what I'm really trying to say is that you've got to make up your mind just where you want this thing between us to go.'

'Isn't that a little—a little *calculated*?' she asked. 'I mean, why can't we just let things happen?'

'My God, teacher! he exploded. 'What do you think' "just happened" here tonight? Or last Saturday at the dance?' He reached out and grabbed her, shaking her slightly. 'I think you're attracted to me, and I know damned good and well that I'm attracted to you. Physically, to be blunt about it. Now, since we both know that, what's the point of fooling around about it?'

'I see,' she said in a tight voice. 'In other words, what's to stop us from hopping into bed immediately?'

'Well, that's putting it in rather crass terms, but yes. That's pretty much the size of it.'

She gave him a long, searching look. 'Is it really that simple to you, Jake?' she asked softly. 'I admit I've led a fairly sheltered life in comparison to yours, or even to most women's these days. And I admit that books have been an important part of my life. But I haven't lived in a cave. I know that relationships between men and women have a strong physical element. And as you said, I feel it myself. But I'll never believe that's *all* there is to it.'

'I never said it was,' he said rather sulkily.

'You certainly implied it.'

He didn't say anything for a long time, just sat staring broodingly through the front windscreen, his fingers lightly tapping on the steering wheel. The enormous, bright yellow moon was high in the night sky now, and shining directly on to his face, which was set in a fierce scowl of concentration.

Claire held her breath, watching him. She didn't want to lose him. Even though every word he uttered clearly revealed a basic philosophy that was diametrically opposed to hers, and even though she knew without a doubt now that he was indeed only playing a game with her, involving her in a contest of wills, she simply couldn't turn her back on him or dismiss him.

What she was prepared to do, however, was resist him as long as possible. She accepted that whatever happened it would end in her defeat, that whether she resisted him or gave in to him she would lose him eventually. She just couldn't make it too easy for him, and that meant she had to risk losing him now, tonight.

Finally, he heaved a deep sigh and turned to her. 'Stubborn little thing, aren't you?' he said in a dry tone. 'If I read you right, what you're saying is that you don't want to rush into anything. Right?'

Relief rolled over her in waves. She'd won. 'Right,' she said. 'Can't we just get to know each other a little better before we—um—get too carried away?'

'OK,' he said, settling back against the car door and folding his arms across his chest. 'Why don't you tell me a little about yourself.'

'Oh, Jake!' she cried, laughing. 'You're incorrigible.' She reached for her door-handle and pressed the latch. 'Now, I've really got to go in. The neighbours will start snooping any minute.'

He walked with her up the path, one arm loosely around her shoulders. At the door, he took her in his arms and gave her a warm, tender kiss. She longed to throw her arms around his neck and press herself up against him, to bring him inside, into her bed, but she'd won an important victory tonight, and she wasn't going to let go of her advantage before she absolutely had to.

It was clearer to her than ever that the only way to hold his interest was to keep him at bay for as long as possible. It wouldn't be easy, and in the end he'd go anyway, but, whatever lay ahead, he would leave her with a memory to cherish for the rest of her life.

CHAPTER SIX

THREE weeks later, on a Thursday night, Claire had dinner with her friends as usual. It was her turn this time, and she'd chosen the small Greek restaurant where she and Curtis had had their last dinner date. It was close to the college, inexpensive, and the food was always excellent.

She'd been delayed by a last-minute conference with one of her students, and was the last one to arrive. The others had already ordered dinner and were drinking their cocktails when she came inside, still out of breath from the five-block walk.

As she threaded her way around the other tables, dodging waitresses laden with trays of food, she had the uneasy feeling that every pair of eyes at her friends' table was fixed on her with undisguised curiosity. By the time she sat down, she was certain of it.

'Sorry I'm late,' she said, and went on to explain the reason for her delay.

When she'd finished, there was dead silence at the table. She looked around from one familiar face to another. Finally, with a nervous laugh, she said, 'Is something wrong?'

Immediately everyone started talking at once. 'Hasn't the weather been atrocious lately?' Deirdre piped up.

'Terrible,' someone else agreed.

'Even for Seattle,' came another voice.

'They say it will snow by Christmas.'

'No, really?'

When the topic of the weather was exhausted, there was a short awkward silence, then someone mentioned the constantly escalating cost of living, and the rest grasped it eagerly. The one thing they all seemed agreed on was to avoid even looking at Claire.

By the time dinner was over, she was ready to scream at them to spit it out. She knew quite well what subject they were all so assiduously avoiding. In the past three weeks she and Jake had been together constantly, sometimes as often as four nights a week. In the course of their wonderings they'd run into at least three of her friends and, at the rate news travelled in the little group, it was common knowledge by now that they were involved in a close relationship.

Kate offered to drive her home, and although Claire knew that would mean a close inquisition she decided she might as well get it over with, and she agreed.

She didn't have to wait long. As soon as Kate had pulled out of the restaurant car park on to the main street, she flicked a glance at Claire and said in an elaborately casual tone, 'I understand you and Jake Donovan have been seen together all over town lately.'

Claire had to smile. 'That's right,' she said briefly.

Kate darted her a swift glance. 'Is that all you have to say?' It was Kate at her most severely accusing.

'What more *can* I say?' Claire asked innocently. 'Do you have any objections?'

'As a matter of fact, since you ask, yes, I do,' was the grim reply. 'Claire, you have no idea what you're letting yourself in for by getting involved with that man. He eats little girls like you for breakfast. There's only heartbreak ahead for you, you know that.'

In spite of her amusement, Claire was stung. 'You don't give me credit, do you, Kate?' she asked coolly. 'Has it ever occurred to you that Jake just might possibly like me, or consider me good company, or find me attractive? It is within the realm of possibility, you know, and not totally out of the question.'

'Of course I think he finds you attractive!' Kate exploded. 'That's just the point. Don't you see? It has nothing to do with you. You could be Helen of Troy and Madame Curie rolled into one, and all a man like Jake Donovan would see is another trophy.'

'I see,' Claire said tightly. 'And you feel it's your duty to warn me off, is that it?'

When they had stopped at the next light, Kate turned to her and gave her a look of genuine concern. 'Please don't be offended, Claire,' she said seriously. 'I know I get out of line sometimes, and push into affairs that are none of my business, but this time I really am worried. I don't want to see you get hurt.'

'Why do you automatically assume that's what will happen?' Claire cried in exasperation. 'That's what you all assume, isn't it? That's why none of you would even look at me tonight, much less ask me nicely about Jake. It's not a guilty secret, for heaven's sake. We like each other, we're attracted to each other.

What's so wrong about that?'

Kate didn't say anything after that, and every time Claire glanced her way she saw the same tight-lipped frown on her face. It wasn't until she'd parked at the kerb in front of Claire's building that she spoke again.

'All right, Claire,' she said. 'Maybe I was out of line, but please don't be mad at me. I guess I've always felt a little protective towards you. You were always such a dreamy kid, so out of touch with the harsh facts of life, especially after your mother died and your father left Seattle. But you're right. It's time I let go the apron strings. You're a big girl. You can take care of yourself. Now, are we still friends?'

'Oh, of course we are. I know your intentions are the best, Kate, and I know you only do these things because you care about me.'

'Then let me say just one thing more, and you'll never hear another word on the subject from me.' She hesitated, and when Claire kept silent, went on, 'Everybody knows Jake Donovan's reputation with women. Love 'em and leave 'em, that's the way he operates. I've even heard rumours that he has some kind of game plan he follows that boils the art of seduction down to a science. If you've got any sense at all, you'll run from him as fast as you can. Do you honestly think you can handle that kind of calculated determination and not get burned?'

'Yes,' Claire said, still a little irritated. 'I can.'

Kate sighed. 'Then more power to you. I know I couldn't.'

Claire made a noise of disgust. 'And as for all these rumours you've been hearing, that's all they are.

No one knows what he's really like, not the way I do.'

Kate nodded owlishly. 'Oh, I see,' she drawled. 'The real Jake Donovan is a pussycat you've already got eating out of your hand. Is that it?'

Claire shifted uncomfortably in her seat. 'I didn't say that,' she replied stiffly. 'I just don't like people spreading stories about a man they don't even know.'

'If you're implying . . .' Kate began with fire in her eyes.

'Oh, *please*, Kate!' Can't we just drop the subject?'

Kate had the good grace to close her mouth and clamp her jaw shut, as though physically bottling up the flow that was still on her tongue. She gave Claire one long, searching look, then reached down to turn the key in the ignition.

'OK. I get the message. And I'm sorry, all right? It won't happen again.'

'Kate, please don't be mad.'

'I'm not. You're right. I should mind my own business. And don't worry. Our friendship has survived worse than this. Remember the time you told Sister Ursula I'd copied your paper on that French test and I had to stay after school for a solid week?'

Claire nodded. 'Or the time you fixed me up a blind date with that lecherous cousin of yours who almost raped me?'

The two friends grinned at each other.

Although Claire fully intended to dismiss Kate's sermon on Jake's character as just another example of her compulsion to interfere in the lives of *all* her friends, she found in the days that followed that that wasn't so easy to do.

She couldn't quite dismiss the uneasy suspicion that Kate's warning had only confirmed the nagging doubts in her own mind about the wisdom of continuing a relationship whose only possible consequence to her was a broken heart.

She had a dinner date with Jake the following Saturday night, and he had tickets to a hockey game afterwards. Half a dozen times that day, Claire arrived at the firm conviction that she would break if off with him that very night, while she still had the courage to do it.

But the moment she opened her door to him and saw him standing there, his face ruddy with cold, his overcoat collar turned up to the back of his neck, his green eyes sparkling, all her resolve failed her. He was becoming indispensable to her, and she was helpless against the irresistible force that kept her from doing what she knew was in her own best interests.

'Come in,' she said, opening the door wide. 'You look as if you're about frozen.'

He stepped inside, shedding his coat and throwing it over a chair on the way. When he reached her, he held his arms wide, and as she sank against him all her doubts fled. This was where she wanted to be, and that was all there was to it.

'Mmm, you smell good,' he murmured, nuzzling at her ear. His hands began to travel over her back. 'Maybe we should skip dinner.'

She drew away and gave him a quizzical look. 'I can see you missing dinner, but not the hockey game.'

'Well, you're right there,' he said, releasing her.

Suddenly, she felt a slight prick of irritation. Why was it they always ended up at a hockey game, or a basket ball tournament, or one more dreary, incomprehensible football game? She never knew what was going on, and Jake was always so absorbed in the action that he never bothered to explain anything to her.

'I'll just get my coat,' she said stiffly.

As she walked down the hall to her bedroom, her irritation began to escalate into a full-blown resentment. It seemed that all he wanted of her was a silent companion at his stupid sports events and a potential bed partner. What kind of relationship was that?

By the time she'd taken her coat out of the wardrobe and carried it back into the living-room, she was ready to do battle. Then, when she saw him down on his haunches before her television set, engrossed in watching a tennis match, she simply exploded.

'Jake,' she called to him, 'I want to talk to you.'

'Just a second, Claire,' he said absently over his shoulder. 'I want to catch the National League scores.'

'Jake!' she shouted, stamping her foot. 'I mean now.'

He rose slowly to his feet and turned around to face her, his eyes wide with surprise. 'What's wrong?'

She marched past him to the television set and switched it off with a jerk. Then, with her hands on her hips, she strode over to where he was still standing and glared up at him. The look of total bewilderment on his face only inflamed her anger. She couldn't even speak. Damn it, how could he be so dense, so crass and unfeeling, so thoughtless and . . .

'Are you going to tell me what's wrong?' he said mildly at last. 'Or are you going to make me guess?'

She struggled for control. 'I was just wondering,' she finally bit out, 'why every single evening we spend together *must* revolve around some sports event.'

He reached up a hand and rubbed it over the back of his neck. 'Well, I don't know. I guess it doesn't. It just always seems to work out that way.'

'Has it ever occurred to you that I might enjoy going to a play or an opera or a concert—or even a bad movie?' She spread her arms wide in a dramatic gesture. '*Anything*, at this point, except one more stupid game!'

Their eyes locked together, until Claire felt the sudden hot tears stinging behind her lids. She bit her lip and looked away. He didn't say anything for a long time, and she stood there, staring down at the floor, waiting for him to stalk out of the door, and out of her life for good.

'OK, Claire,' he said. 'Now do you want to tell me what this is really all about?'

'I don't know what you're talking about,' she mumbled.

'Oh, yes, you do. You know damned good and well that all you had to do was tell me what you wanted to do, and I would have been glad to go along with it. In fact, every time I've called you, I've asked you just that. And do you know what your answer has always been? I'll tell you. "Oh, I don't care, Jake," ' he mimicked. ' "Whatever you like." '

Hot waves of shame washed over her, and she could feel her cheeks burning. He was right, of course. It had been exactly like that all along. She couldn't look at him. What had possessed her to accuse him of something she knew quite well he'd never done?

Then he spoke again, in a more reasonable tone. 'Listen, Claire, if you're trying to pick a fight with me as an excuse to get rid of me, why don't you just come out and say so? This silly rigmarole isn't the way to go about it.'

Panic-stricken, she whirled around to face him. 'No!' she cried. 'I don't want that.' She put her arms around his waist and rested her head on his chest. 'I'm sorry. I don't know what got into me. Maybe it's because of the lecture I got the other night from Kate Dawson.'

'About me?' She nodded mutely against his chest. 'Just what horrible things did she have to say about me?' he asked lightly. 'She must have painted me as some kind of monster.'

Claire looked up at him and forced a weak smile. 'Oh, she only wanted to warn me against "that kind of man".'

He sobered instantly. 'Maybe you should listen to her,' he said softly.

Once again the sickening panic rose up in her. 'What do you mean?'

'I only mean that you should be clear about what's going on here.' He put a hand on her cheek. 'I like you, Claire, I really do. And I've made no secret of the fact that I want you badly. But you should be perfectly clear on one thing before this goes any further. I'm not a man to make permanent commitments. I like my life the way it is, and have no intention of changing it, not even for you.'

'I know that, Jake,' she said.

'So if you don't think you can handle that, then now's the time to say so,' he went on as though he hadn't even heard her. 'I don't ever want to mislead you into thinking I'm interested in anything but having a good time. I'm not particularly proud of that,' he added hastily. 'Nor do I consider it a very lofty ambition,but it's the way I am, the way I want to live.'

Well, she thought, he couldn't make it any plainer than that. She'd known it all along anyway, but somehow she found it profoundly depressing to hear him spell it out so explicitly. In spite of all her warnings to herself, she had to admit now that all along she'd nursed a secret hope that he might change.

Now she knew he wouldn't. She could take it or leave it. There wasn't a doubt in her mind that if she pressed the issue, he would turn and walk out of her life forever. He was also honest about his determination to get her into bed eventually, and she knew that when that happened it would be the end. The longer she held out against him, the longer he would stay with her.

She smiled up at him. 'I'm a big girl, Jake. And havinga good time together is all I want, too.'

He leaned down and kissed her lightly on the mouth. 'Well, then, what shall it be? The hockey game or a bad movie?'

She laughed. 'I'll concede the hockey game tonight,

since you already have the tickets. But next time it'll be my turn to choose. Fair enough?'

He nodded. 'Fair enough.'

The status quo continued on into Decemeber, with no remarkable change in the relationship except that now, on their evenings out, Claire suggested alternatives to the endless sports events. True to his word, Jake went along good-naturedly with everything she wanted to do, and even seemed to enjoy most of it, with the possible exception of one long, boring Russian play at the Repertory Theatre.

Also true to his word, he continued pressing her to go to bed with him, and she just as firmly continued to resist. She really had to admire his patience and his indomitable will. He never grew angry when she called a halt to their lovemaking, but the next time out he would once again push it as far as she would allow.

It was the middle of December now, and the college was on its annual two-week holiday between terms. On the Saturday night before Christmas, Jake had taken her out to dinner and then to a film, which they both agreed was bad. Afterwards, in her apartment, Claire steeled herself for another battle of wills on the couch, when, to her surprise, he sat down on the chair opposite her and lit a cigarette.

'What are your plans for Christmas?' he asked.

'I don't know. I usually go up to Camano Island to stay with my father.'

'How would you like to drive over to Yakima with me and spend a few days with my sister and her family? We can come back on Christmas Day, if you like, so you can still visit your father.'

Claire stared at him. 'I didn't even know you had a sister.'

'Oh, I keep her well-hidden,' he said with a grin.

She was completely taken aback by the unexpected offer. Did it mean that his feelings for her ran deeper than he cared to admit, even to himself? Nothing had happened beteeen them since their last discussion that would make her think so, but with Jake you never knew. He played his cards close to his chest, always. Stay cool, she warned herself, don't jump to conclusions.

'Well, yes,' she said at last in a light, casual tone. 'That sounds like fun. I'm sure my father will understand.'

It was on the tip of her tongue to suggest that he go with her to her father's when they got back, but she stopped herself just in time. He'd made an enormous concession, she was sure, in asking her to meet his sister. If she pressed the family issue now, he might think she was taking more for granted than he intended.

'Good,' he said. 'I think you'll like Linda. She's as strait-laced as you are. You two should get along just fine.'

'Tell me about her and her family,' she said. 'What does her husband do?'

'She's a widow. Cliff was killed in a car accident about three years ago.'

'How old are her children?'

He scratched his head and grinned at her. 'Damned if I know. 'Timmy just started school, so he must be six or seven, Jennifer was born right after Cliff died, so she can't be more than three.'

'It must be hard for her, raising two children on her own.'

'She does a great job, though. Cliff left her well provided for, so she only has to work part-time. She's a nurse-practitioner and can pretty much choose her own hours.'

He rose to his feet and crossed over to the couch, reaching up to switch off the lamp as he settled down beside her. 'Now,' he said, reaching for her, 'is tonight the night?'

'Afraid not,' she said.

'We'll see about that,' he murmured as he drew her into his arms and pressed his lips against her neck.

'You never give up, do you?' she said with a sigh.

'Nope,' he said, nipping lightly at the skin of her neck and chin. 'And I never will.'

I hope you mean that, she prayed silently. Then, as his seeking mouth found hers and one hand settled over her breast, all thought vanished and she gave herself up to the sheer pleasure of his arms around her, his hard body pressed against hers.

Christmas fell on a Wednesday, and so they left Seattle early on Monday morning. As everyone had been predicting for weeks, they did have snow and, although only traces fell in the city, it became heavier and heavier as they climbed up the west side of the Cascade Mountains towards Snoqualmie Pass. However, the wide highway over the summit was kept well-cleared, and the Mercedes purred along at a good speed.

It was only an hour to the pass, then down the eastern slope to the flat lands beyond, all blanketed with snow. They passed through the few small towns along the way, then in another hour turned off the interstate on to the narrow road that led to the thriving farming community of Yakima, famous for its apple orchards.

Jake's sister lived on the outskirts of town in a rambling old two-storey house set in an acre of ground. Although it had stopped snowing by the time they pulled into the driveway, there were heavy drifts against the house, and in the front garden were two small children, dressed warmly and with bright red caps on their heads, playing in the snow. When they saw the car, they both came running over, shouting at the top of their lungs.

'Uncle Jake!' Uncle Jake!' they cried, clamouring at his door.

He jumped out of the car, scooped them both up together in his arms and held them up as they wriggled with pleasure. As Claire got out on her side, a slim young woman dressed in warm trousers and a ski parka appeared on the porch of the house, one hand over her eyes to protect them from the glare of the midday sun, the other waving.

'You made good time,' she called, walking towards them. She turned to Claire and held out a hand. 'You must be Claire Talbot. Hi, I'm Linda. I'm so glad you could come.' She gave her brother a fond glance. 'I suppose he drove like a maniac, as usual.'

Jake set the children down and put an arm around

his sister. 'I resent that,' he complained, dropping a kiss on her forehead. 'I was the epitome of prudence. Even you would have felt safe with me.'

'Come on inside. I have lunch all ready.'

Claire helped Linda with the dishes after the hearty, warming meal of thick home-made soup and toasted sandwiches, while Jake went outside with the children to help them build a snowman.

She had warmed to Linda immediately, and felt at home in the large, rather shabby house, filled with the paraphernalia of children, and making no pretence at elegant décor.

The two women chatted easily as they worked, about their respective jobs mostly, but Claire's eyes were constantly drawn to the kitchen window, where she had a clear view of Jake playing in the snow with the children.

Linda came up to the counter with a tray of dishes, and, as her gaze followed Claire's, she laughed indulgently. 'He's still a big kid himself in many ways, isn't he?'

Claire smiled at her. 'I must say I'm rather surprised. Somehow I never thought of Jake as being good with children.'

'Oh, they adore him. He's been like a father to them since Cliff was killed. And from the way he describes his work in coaching, I'd guess he handles his players with the same kind of affection and discipline.'

'You're right,' Claire said slowly. 'I never thought of it in quite that way.'

Linda turned away and started rinsing off dishes.

'I always thought Jake would be a wonderful father to his own children,' she said in an offhand tone.

Claire had no reply to that. Seeing this new side of the man had taken her so by surprise that she didn't know what to think.

The days passed quickly. As Jake had predicted, Claire did indeed like Linda, very much. She treated Jake as most sisters did their older brothers, with a combination of fond indulgence and tart criticism. The most astounding part of the whole visit, though, was to watch Jake with his niece and nephew.

For some reason, Claire had had the idea that Jake detested children. He had never mentioned his sister's family and, given his determined avoidance of matrimony, she had assumed it was probably largely because he didn't want to be bothered with children. It came as a real surprise to her, then, to see the genuine interest he took in them the whole time they were there.

On Tusesday, after lunch, Jake took the children to town to visit Santa Claus at a local department store, while the two women got out lights and ornaments and started to trim the Christmas tree.

Linda perched herself up on the step-ladder to work on the higher branches, while Claire fastened the lights around the bottom. They worked silently for half an hour when suddenly, out of the blue, Linda said, 'I'm so glad you could come with Jake. It's the first time he's ever brought one of his women friends here. I was beginning to wonder if he was ashamed of me and the children.'

Claire paused and looked up at her. 'I hardly think that. It's certainly obvious to me how much he cares about all of you.'

Linda stepped down from the ladder and picked up a string of lights. Then, very carefully, she said, 'Claire, would you be offended if I asked you a very personal question?'

'No, not at all.'

'I've been wondering just how serious you and Jake are.'

Claire thought a minute. 'To be perfectly honest, I'd have to say we aren't.' She laughed lightly. 'I don't think Jake has it in him to be serious about a woman.'

Linda gave her a quizzical look, then said slowly, 'Well, I probably shouldn't be telling you this—and don't you ever dare mention to him that I did or he'll kill me—but Jake was serious about a woman just once in his life that I know of, and I think Sandra probably cured him forever.'

Claire's heart stopped beating, then turned over and began to hammer erratically. 'Sandra?' she asked.

'Yes. He and Sandra were childhood sweethearts, grew up together right here in Yakima. They married when they graduated from college, both of them too young.'

'What happened?'

Linda shrugged and climbed back up on the ladder. 'The usual thing,' she called down to her. 'Jake started making a lot of money in pro ball, but he was also on the road a lot, and when a team is in training the players are expected to live together, separated from their wives. This left Sandra free as the breeze, and apparently she took it upon herself to entertain the entire team behind Jake's back, including his best friend, whom she later married.'

Claire was speechless. It explained so much about him. If he had been that badly burned in the past, she could see how it might turn even the most idealistic young man into a calculating machine who could never trust a woman again.

Then she realised that Linda had descended the ladder again and was standing before her, looking at her with consternation.

'Listen, Claire,' she said. 'I probably shouldn't have said anything. But I like you. And I can see that Jake does, too. You could be just what he needs to get over the past.' She hesitated. 'Now I'm really going to step out of line and ask you a very personal question. You don't have to answer if you don't want to.' She drew in a deep breath. 'Are you in love with him?'

Of course I am, was the unspoken thought. She saw clearly now that she had been all along, only she'd been so sure she'd have to give him up eventually that she hadn't dared to admit it, even to herself.

Now that was all changed. After hearing Linda's story, she no longer saw him as a threat to her, an enemy she had to keep at a safe distance. All she could think of was that now there might be a chance for them, a real future. She looked at Linda, who was still waiting for an answer to her question.

'Yes,' she said. 'I love him.'

'Then go for it,' Linda said with fierce intensity. 'I'd hate to see him let you get away.'

* * *

Christmas morning dawned bright, clear and cold. They planned to leave early in order to reach Seattle in time for Claire to visit her father, and after a large breakfast it was time to leave. While Jake went out to pack the car, Linda and Claire cleared up.

When they were ready and had walked outside, the bonnet of the car was raised, and Jake was peering inside at the engine. Then he slammed the bonnet shut and stood wiping his hands on his handkerchief, frowning down at the car.

'Is something wrong?' Claire asked as she came towards him.

'It looks as though I might have a loose fan belt,' he said. Then he smiled. 'But let's not worry about that now. I doubt if any garage will be open today, and we can probably make it as far as Seattle. Are you ready to go?'

They said their goodbyes then, with promises to visit again soon, and drove off. It was a fine, sunny day, the roads were clear, and as they drove westwards through the fields of snow towards the mountains, Claire sat quietly beside him, still pondering the conversation she'd had with Jake's sister, and what it might mean to their relationship.

It was warm and cosy in the luxurious interior. The radio was playing Christmas carols, and Jake was humming along with them under his breath. After they had gone some way, he turned to her.

'Well,' he said, 'how did you enjoy your Christmas?'

'Oh, it was wonderful, Jake.' She held out her hand, where an expensive platinum watch sparkled on her wrist. 'And I love my watch. Although it must have cost the earth.'

'Ah, nothing is too good for my girl,' he joked, waggling his heavy, dark eyebrows. He reached out an arm to pull her towards him, and she snuggled happily up against him.

Soon they had left the last town behind and started up the eastern slope of the mountains towards the pass. As the ascent became steeper, an ominous flapping noise began to issue from under the bonnet of the Mercedes.

Jake swore softly under his breath. 'I was afraid of that,' he muttered, glowering. 'Damn it, I should have tried to get it checked before we left. I think that loose fan belt just died.'

Then, miraculously, just around the next bend, a tiny roadsider service station appeared, a row of shabby wooden cabins stretching behind it. The car was limping badly now, and they made it off the highway just as it stopped altogether.

He gave her a rueful look. 'With luck, I might be able to get the belt replaced here,' he said as he stepped outside. 'If so, it'll only take a few minutes.'

She smiled at him. 'Well, then, I wish you luck.'

He walked off towards the garage, where a short, stocky man in greasy overalls and a baseball cap was tinkering with the engine of a battered pick-up truck. Jake spoke to him, gesturing towards the Mercedes. Then the mechanic shook his head slowly. After a few more moments of conversation, Jake came back and leaned down to speak to her through the open window.

'I'm sorry, Claire. He doesn't have a fan belt to fit. His helper is gone over the holidays, and he won't be able to pick up a new one until tomorrow.'

'Tomorrow?' she said. 'What does that mean?'

'I'm afraid it means we'll have to spend the night here.'

CHAPTER SEVEN

'THE problem is,' he went on hurriedly, 'there's only one cabin left. And we're lucky to get that one. Seems there was a last-minute cancellation just before we got here.'

Their eyes met briefly. As it sank in just what that meant, Claire's mind raced. He had her trapped, and for one second all her old wariness returned. But, over the past few days, her feelings for him had altered in such a fundamental way that she couldn't really sustain her suspicions of him for long. His sister's story about his past and seeing him with his niece and nephew had made an enormous difference to her, forcing her to admit how much she loved him and wanted him herself, all of him.

'Well, then,' she said finally with a reassuring smile. 'We'll just have to make the best of it.'

The look of relief on his face was almost funny, and she had to hide her smile as he opened the door for her and she got out to stand beside him.

'Tell you what,' he said. 'For being such a good sport about it, I'll buy you a cup of coffee.'

In spite of their predicament, Claire was entranced by the beauty of their surroundings. They were a little less then half-way to the summit by now, and the terrain was already mountainous, with towering snow-laden conifers as far as the eye could see. She could hear the sound of rushing water nearby, and while Jake went over to the machine to get their coffee, she wandered out to the back of the garage to investigate.

As she turned the corner, one of the most beautiful sights she had ever seen was suddenly spread out before her. Down the snowy slope was a creek bed, fed by the springs in the mountains, and on the other side stood a mother deer with two fawns.

Moving carefully, so as not to startle them, she inched her way down the bank of the stream. It was so clear that the flat rocks at the bottom were visible. She stood there, motionless, watching the deer, and listening to the gurgling water, the tap of a woodpecker high in a nearby Douglas fir.

When Jake appeared behind her, she turned her head around carefully. 'Look, Jake,' she said in a hushed voice, pointing to the deer. 'Isn't that a perfectly lovely sight?'

He gazed at her for a moment without speaking, the coffee-cups steaming in his hands, then shifted his eyes to the scene beyond her. 'Yes,' he said quietly. 'It's very lovely.'

Silently he handed her the coffee, and they stood together in the snow without speaking. The silent communion between them, all alone on the mountain-side, was intensely moving to Claire, and she had never felt so close to him as she did at that moment.

Then a voice called out. 'Mr Donovan.' It was the mechanic. They turned to see him waving. 'I've got your key for you if you want to get settled. It's cabin number six, down at the end.'

Jake went up to get the key from him, then came back and handed it to her. 'Why don't you go and take a look while I get the bags from the car?'

Inside the cabin there was only one small living-room, with a tiny bathroom and miniature kitchen facilities in front of the window. Behind the opposite wall, a long, low couch. The room was freezing cold, but a fire was laid in the rough hearth.

When Jake appeared a few minutes later with their bags, he set them down just inside the door and stood there silently, his eyes making a broad survey of the cramped, shabby room.

'Well,' he said at last. 'It doesn't look much, does it? Think you can put up with it for one night?'

'Oh, it's not so bad,' she said. 'Why don't you light the fire? That should cheer things up a bit.'

Still he made no sign of moving. She gave him an enquiring look. 'Jake? What's wrong?'

To her astonishment, his face went brick-red. 'I was just wondering about the—er—the sleeping arrangements,' he said in a hesitant voice. Then he went on more briskly, 'How about if you take the bed, and I use the couch?'

She hesitated. He was obviously leaving it up to her. The mere fact that he had offered her that option tipped the scales. She took a deep breath, crossed over to where he stood and looked up at him. 'All right, Jake,' she said calmly. 'If that's what you want.'

His dark eyebrows shot up, and he stared down at her for several seconds. Then he put his hand on her shoulders, the green eyes still boring into hers.

'Are you saying what I think you're saying?' he asked in a low voice. 'You're not just . . .'

She raised a finger and put it on his lips. 'You light the fire, and I'll go see if our friend has something in the way of food for at least one meal.'

'I'm not really hungry,' he said huskily. His mouth crooked in a smile and he pulled her closer. 'That was an enormous breakfast Linda gave us.'

She drew away from him. So long as she had made up her mind what she was going to do, it wouldn't hurt to make him wait. 'Fire and food first,' she said sternly. 'Then maybe we can take a walk.'

'You're a hard woman,' he said, but he did as she asked and crossed over to get the fire started.

Claire was able to wheedle a few cans of soup and a box of crackers from the dour mechanic. It was hardly a Christmas meal, but Claire knew this Christmas would be special in a different, more important way. Ater they'd eaten, they decided to go for a walk. She was still a little apprehensive about what lay ahead, and wanted to delay it as long as possible while she got used to the idea.

They strolled along hand in hand for some distance beside the banks of the stream, hardly speaking except to comment on the scenery, and by the time they headed back the sun was setting fast. Soon it would be dark. As they walked through the growing twilight, their booted feet crunching in the snow, Claire felt herself to be in a strangely transfixed mental state, and was grateful for the silence.

When they arrived back at the cabin, the mechanic

was walking away from the front porch, where he had just dumped a load of fresh firewood.

'You go on inside, Claire,' Jake said. 'I want to have a word with him about the repairs.'

He called out, and Claire stood by the door for a moment, watching him in the gathering dusk as he spoke to the other man, his stance relaxed, his expression serious. He was such an impressive-looking man, with his air of assurance, his tall strength, and she thought she had never loved him so much as she did at that minute.

Inside the cabin, the hot coals were still smouldering where Jake had banked the fire before they left, and the room was warm at last. Claire took off her jacket and went to stand in front of it, warming her hands. In a moment, she heard Jake's step on the porch, the stamp of his feet, the click of the latch, and her heart stood still as he came up behind her.

Without speaking, he reached out for her, turned her around and pulled her roughly into his arms, holding her tightly against him. Claire could feel the pounding of his heart under hers, his warm breath on her face.

'God, Claire,' he murmured in her ear. 'I've wanted to do this all afternoon.'

An overpowering surge of love and desire welled up in her at his words. The abrupt contrast in him between his silent distance that afternoon and this eager, passionate lover excited her beyond words. His hands moved down to her hips, pulling her lower body closer to his, and she was left in no doubt about the reality and urgency of his desire. She raised her face for his kiss, and his hot mouth came down on hers.

Finally, reluctantly, he tore his lips from hers and raised his head. 'I can't wait any longer,' he muttered. 'I'm so greedy for you, all of you.'

'I know, Jake,' she whispered. 'I want you, too.'

He reached out a hand to touch her face, and in the half-light cast by the glowing coals she saw the earnest expression on his lean face. 'I want you to know, Claire,' he said gravely, 'that I do care about you. I'll never lie to you, and I'll never wilfully harm you in any way.'

She believed him absolutely. He'd always been open about his feelings in the past, and she knew he always would be. That was all she could ask of him now. The choice was hers. There were no guarantees that she would ever possess him entirely, but now she at least felt there was hope.

As he rubbed his thumb over her mouth, Claire could feel the tension, the warmth, the desire slowly building up between them. An insistent heat spread through her, and she raised her arms up around his neck.

'I know,' she murmured. 'It's all right.' She hesitated. What she wanted most in the world at that moment was to tell him how much she loved him, but her old habit of caution made her remain silent.

He kissed her again, a deep, tender kiss that filled her with joy and seemed to put the final seal on their tacit understanding. She pressed herself against his long, hard, masculine body in a gesture of total surrender, free now to give herself to him without fear.

'Let's sit in front of the fire,' he murmured in her ear. 'There's something I've wanted to do since the first moment we met.'

He threw on some fresh logs, and when they had settled themselves on the rug in front of the rekindled blaze he turned to her. She waited breathlessly, wondering what was coming. Then he raised his hands to her hair and slowly began to take out the pins, laying them one by one carefully on the brick hearth.

This slow, deliberate operation only fuelled her longing. It was as though he was undressing her, and by the time the last pin was removed she was breathing shallowly, her lips parted, almost faint with desire and anticipation. The heavy coil of hair had fallen over her shoulders, and he was parting the smooth strands now with deft fingers until it hung in a silken curtain around her face.

His glowing green eyes bored into her as he stroked the long auburn mane back from her forehead. 'I knew it,' he breathed. 'I knew you'd be even more beautiful this way.'

Her heart was pounding wildly, and there was a choking sensation in her throat. She couldn't speak. Hardly able even to breathe, she watched as his head bent slowly towards her.

He kissed her again, deeply, urgently, with one arm around her shoulders. His other hand came to rest on her breast, and she felt herself being eased backwards against the couch directly behind them. His tongue penetrated past her parted lips, and when his hand slipped inside her blouse to touch her bare flesh her last doubt vanished in the thrill of the sensations his touch aroused in her.

There was no question in her mind now. She clutched at him as he raised his head, tearing his mouth from hers so that he could speak. 'Come,' he said. Without a word, she allowed him to raise her to her feet.

More floating then walking, she followed him over to the sleeping alcove. He drew aside the curtain to reveal the wide bed, then took her in his arms and held her gently. After a few moments, he cupped her chin in his hand and tilted her head back to look deeply down into her eyes. Still holding her gaze in his, he slowly began to unfasten her blouse.

When the last button was undone, he spread the material aside and bent his head to place his lips on her bare shoulder. Claire leaned down and pressed her cheek against the dark head, her arms around him, cradling him to her as his mouth moved to the crook of her neck, her other shoulder, and he began to tug gently but insistently at the straps of her lacy bra.

She held her breath as both large, warm hands began to move over her bare breasts, kneading gently in a slow rotating motion. Instinctively, she reached out to unfasten his shirt and reach inside to run her hands over his smooth, bare, muscled chest, where she could feel the heavy, erratic thud of his heartbeat.

In one deft movement, he shrugged out of the shirt and pulled her up against him. His hands were everywhere now, in a frenzy of passion, on her breasts, her stomach, her back, sliding down underneath the loosened waistband of her trousers to clutch at her hips, and as he pulled her against his hard body she gasped aloud at his unmistakable, thrusting need.

A sudden awareness of her own power over him came to her then, awesome in its intensity. Her knees weakened, threatening to buckle under her, and he eased her down on to the bed. She slumped limply back on the pillow, her head whirling crazily, her pounding heart about to burst.

She raised her hips so that he could pull off the rest of her clothing, then closed her eyes and waited for him while he finished undressing. When his body finally came down to cover hers, she clung to him blindly. His hands and mouth continued to work their magic on her eager body, nuzzling and stroking her to a point of terrible aching need, until finally she cried out to him and they were joined together at last.

For the first time in her life, Claire went to sleep in a man's arms and woke up with him beside her in the bed.

She had slept deeply, dreamlessly, completely sated by Jake's expert lovemaking. It wasn't until the first early-morning light filtered in through the thin curtains at the window that her eyes fluttered open and she gradually awakened.

In the first instant of consciousness, memory came flooding back, warming her. Lying on her back, she was intensely, vividly aware of the long, hard body lying next to hers. She gazed over at him, needing to see him, to assure herself he was still there.

He was sleeping quietly, his dark head turned away from her, his arms and shoulders outside the covers.

She stared at the broad planes of his chest and shoulders, smoothly muscled, not a spare ounce of flesh on him. They were not quite touching, and, as Claire watched the steady rise and fall of his chest, she shifted her position slightly, hardly moving at all, just to feel his bare skin against hers again, the body so different from her own.

Immediately, the rhythm of his breathing changed. He went quite still for a moment, then opened one sleepy eye and slowly turned to face her. He grunted contentedly and reached out a hand to touch the hair still streaming over her bare shoulders.

'Good morning,' he said in a low voice. He opened both eyes and raised himself up on one elbow to gaze down at her. Then he smiled and kissed her lightly on the mouth. 'How are you?'

She returned his smile. 'Wonderful,' she replied.

His expression grew grave. 'Why didn't you tell me, Claire? If I'd known it was the first time . . .' He broke off and shook his head slowly. 'God, it's hard to believe that a woman could reach the ripe old age of twenty-four in this day and age without any experience at all.' He frowned. 'Why didn't you tell me?'

She put a hand on his face. 'Would it really have made any differnece?' she asked softly.

'I don't know,' he said. 'I honestly don't know.' He gave her a rueful smile. 'I only know how badly I wanted you.'

She raised her arms and clasped her hands around his neck. 'Well, I felt the same way. It was my decision. I may be inexperienced, but I'm not a child, after all. I'm a responsible adult, a mature woman.'

The green eyes glinted appreciatively. 'That you are,' he murmured, and lowered his head to kiss her.

His large hands began to travel over her, and as his mouth moved to her breast she clutched his tousled dark head in her hands, pressing it to her. His unshaven face rasped deliciously on her bare skin, creating a sensuous blend of pain and pleasure that sent her soaring to the heights of passion once again.

By the time they'd had a meagre breakfast consisting of another can of soup and more stale crackers, the owner's helper had arrived with the new fan belt for the Mercedes.

While Jake went outside to see to the car, Claire straightened up the cabin and repacked her bag. When she had finished, she gave the cold, dingy little room one last, lingering glance. It wasn't much of a romantic love-nest, but it would always hold a special place in her heart for the wonderful memories it held.

Locking the door behind her, she went outside into the freezing cold. Dark clouds were threatening, and she shivered a little, even in her heavy jacket. Snow in the mountains usually meant rain in Seattle, and she had been hoping for another pleasant sunny day for the trip home.

The bonnet was still raised on the Mercedes, and Jake seemed to be so intent on watching the helper's operation that Claire decided not to bother him. She could return the key herself to the owner, who was in the garage, bent over another repair job.

She walked over to him. 'Here's the key to the

cabin.'

He straightened up and took it from her with a brief nod. 'Hope you had a comfortable night, Mrs Donovan.'

Mrs Donovan? 'Yes,' she said. 'It was fine.'

He pushed his greasy baseball cap back and scratched his head. 'You know, I offered your husband a bigger cabin, but he said he preferred that one, said it would be quieter down there at the end of the line.'

Claire's heart lurched sickeningly, and she stared at the man. 'Yes,' she said stiffly at last. 'It's all right.'

She turned quickly away. She felt like running, she didn't know where, anywhere, so long as it was out of there, away from the scene which had suddenly become so hateful. She needed to be by herself, to think things over. Blindly, she stumbled towards the back of the garage and half slid down the snowy slope to the stream.

She stood there, wringing her hands, the hot tears stinging her eyes, agonising over what she'd just learned. He'd *lied* to her! Jake had told her a deliberate lie, with the sole intention of getting her into bed. Oh, he was so clever! Far too clever for her. What in the world had ever made her imagine she was a match for him, or that she could deal with him openly and honestly?

She almost had to laugh aloud through her tears. To think that she had actually trusted him! The hope that had seemed so promising only yesterday now made her feel a perfect fool, a naïve, gullible, sentimental idiot. She recalled Kate's warning. He'd perfected a game plan when it came to women, all right, and she'd fallen right into the trap.

As she stood there heaping ashes on her head for her stupid behaviour, she also became dimly aware that she had to make a decision. The car would be ready any minute now, and it would be time to leave. He'd come after her.

A blind, unreasoning panic gripped her by the throat, almost choking her. What should she do now? What *could* she do? She was stuck with him, at least until they got back to Seattle. Thank God she hadn't raised the subject of his going with her to visit her father! That was out of the question now, mere romantic fantasy.

Then, suddenly, from the top of the slope, she heard him call to her. 'Claire, we're all set now. Are you ready to go?'

She'd just have to sit it out. Once she was safely home, she'd make some excuse to get rid of him, and then that would be the end of it.

She turned around. 'Yes,' she called back. 'I'm ready.'

It was a tense, silent drive. As they approached the summit, the dark grey sky finally opened up and began to dump snow on them in earnest. Claire was glad of it, since it meant Jake had to give all his attention to keeping the windscreen clear and staying on the road, which grew slushier and slicker by the minute.

'God, I just hope the highway patrol doesn't stop us and make us put on chains,' he muttered at one point.

She didn't reply. She was still too numb with hurt and anger to care what happened to them, and besides, there was nothing to say. By now she wouldn't even have cared if they suddenly started sliding over to the side of the road and plunged into one of the steep ravines on either side.

Gradually, however, as they started down the western slope of the pass, the snow turned to slush, then hard, driving rain. When they reached North Bend, Jake slowed at the crossroads in the centre of town and turned to her.

'Are you hungry? That bowl of soup wasn't much in the way of sustenance. Would you like to stop and have a bite to eat?'

'No, thank you,' she said in a stiff, polite tone.

Her hands were folded tightly in her lap and she couldn't even look at him. She could, however, sense that his eyes were fastened on her in a long, questioning stare.

'Well, would you mind if we stopped anyway?' he asked, equally polite. 'I'm starving.'

She couldn't miss the undertone of irritation in his voice, and she turned to face him. 'Yes, a matter of face I would mind,' she said sharply. 'I should get home and call my father. He'll be worried about me.'

With a sudden jerk and a harsh grinding of gears, the car shot forward, through the crossroads. He didn't say a word, but when she shifted her eyes sideways at him in a covert glance she could see that his face was set and grim, his eyes narrowed, and that a pulse was beating erratically along his bony jaw.

She continued to stare stonily straight ahead. What did he have to be annoyed about? He'd got what he wanted. Little scenarios kept popping into her mind, clever ways of letting him know she'd found out about his little game, but she kept her mouth clamped firmly shut, knowing she was no match for him.

Finally, when they reached the small town of Issaquah, he slowed down and pulled abruptly off the road into the car park in front of a McDonald's restaurant. Well, let him go feed his face, she thought. She didn't care.

Instead of getting out of the car, however, he turned to face her. 'All right, Claire,' he said sternly. 'Out with it. What's wrong?'

'Nothing's wrong.'

'Oh, come on!' he ground out angrily. 'Don't try one of those schoolgirl pouts on me. This isn't Scott you're dealing with, or that dim professor of yours. You've got something on your mind, and I want to hear about it right now.'

'I don't want to talk about it,' she muttered.

'All right,' he said, settling back in his seat and crossing his arms in front of him. 'Then we'll just have to sit here, because I'm not taking you home until you do.'

She was beside herself by now, and uncaring what she said or how it sounded. 'Very well,' she bit out, turning on him. 'Would you care to explain to me just why you lied to me?' She gave a harsh, mirthless laugh. 'Of course, I already know *why* you lied. That's clear enough. What I want to know is how a clever man like you ever thought you'd get away with it.'

He stared blankly at her, then said, 'I haven't the vaguest idea what you're talking about.'

'Oh, no?' she cried. 'Well, let me refresh your memory. You told me we got the only available cabin, that we'd have to share it. And I believed you! That's what really infuriates me.'

'But it *was* the only one available.'

'Then why did the owner tell me this morning that he'd offered you a larger one and you'd turned it done?' she shouted triumphantly.

Slowly his eyes widened as comprehension dawned, and a dark red flush began to spread over his face. He glowered out of the window, his fingers drumming on the steering wheel, and when he turned back to her again, his face was ashen.

'All right,' he said heavily. 'It's true. But that was *after* we were already settled. When we first got there, it *was* the only one vacant. Then, when we came back from our walk and saw the owner with the firewood, he mentioned that a party had left unexpectedly and there was a better cabin available if we wanted it.' He paused, searching her face. 'By then,' he went on in a low voice, 'you'd led me to believe you were as eager as I was to spend the night together. If I was mistaken, I apologise. But there was no malicious intent, and I had no thought of tricking you or deceiving you.'

She didn't know what to say. On the one hand, she still felt used, manipulated, but on the other, his explanation certainly sounded like the truth. If so, he was perfectly within his rights. She *had*, after all, made it clear to him that she was ready to sleep with him.

'Claire,' he said softly, 'do you believe me? I'm telling you the absolute truth.'

'Yes,' she said at last. 'I do believe you. And I'm sorry I jumped to conclusions that way.'

'Then it's all right?'

She met his eyes at last and forced out a bright smile. 'Yes, of course. Everything is fine.'

But it wasn't all right. Somehow the spell had been broken, if not by his deceit, then by her own suspicions, and, although they managed to be civil to each other, they drove the rest of the way in a largely tense, uneasy silence.

When he dropped her off at her apartment, he didn't ask to come in, nor did she invite him. They were both grimy and tired, and, even though the unpleasantness between them had been resolved, it had also effectively dampened the ardour of the night before.

'I can manage by myself,' she said as she retrieved her bag and stepped out of the car into a pouring rain. 'No point in both of us getting soaked.'

He nodded briefly. 'I'll call you,' he said, then drove off without a backward glance.

When she was safely inside her own bedroom at last, the first thing she did was to strip off her grubby clothes and get under a hot shower. Then, with her hair washed, the apartment warm and cosy, she went into the kitchen to make herself a sandwich from the leftover meat loaf in the fridge. She didn't think she'd ever be able to face another can of soup again.

She felt much better after she'd eaten. The rain

was still pelting against the windows. It would be a good day to curl up with a book and laze away the rest of the afternoon. But first she had to call her father. She should have tried to find a telephone yesterday to let him know she wouldn't make it to his place, but all she had had on her mind at that point was Jake.

As she dialled his number and listened to it ring, she felt a sudden longing to see him, and when he answered she was so relieved, she almost burst into tears.

'Dad?' It's Claire. I'm sorry I didn't make it up there yesterday. We had car trouble on the other side of the pass and had to spend the night.'

'Well, I'm glad you're all right,' he said. 'I was a little worried about you.' Then he chuckled. 'But I had a fine holiday. Two of the local widows took me in and fed me, one on Christmas Eve, the other on Christmas Day.'

'Sounds as if you were well taken care of. You'd better watch it, Dad. You're a prime catch, you know.'

'Don't be impertinent, girl,' he said on a note of mock-severity. 'Now, tell me, how was your trip to Yakima?'

'Oh, lots of snow east of the mountains. Very cold. Jake's sister has two children, and that made Christmas fun.'

'And just when am I going to get to meet the famous Jake Donovan?' he asked lightly. 'It's not every day a man's daughter brings home one of the greatest quarterbacks in football history.'

'I'm afraid I can't make it until next weekend,

Dad. Although college doesn't start again until New Year, the teachers have to be back at work on Monday for meetings and preparation. Would next Saturday suit you?'

'That sounds great. Come when you can and stay as long as you like. I'm always happy to see you, honey, you know that, with or without Jake Donovan.'

'Sure I won't put a spanner in the widows' matrimonial schemes?' she asked playfully.

'Goodbye, Claire,' he said firmly. 'I'll see you next Saturday.'

It was only natural that her father, an ardent football fan, would want to meet Jake, she thought after she'd hung up. But she needed to get away on her own, to think things over, and it would do her good to leave town for a few days.

She honestly did believe Jake had told her the truth about the mix-up over the cabins, but what bothered her was her own inability to trust him. What kind of relationship could they possibly have if she jumped to the worst possible conclusion every time her suspicions were aroused?

Still in her robe and slippers, she settled down on the couch with one of her favourite novels, a pot of tea on the table beside her. But she hadn't read two pages before she began glancing at the telephone on the desk, willing it to ring.

On Saturday Claire dutifully started on her preparations for Monday's meeting right after breakfast. Although the work was distracting, she still had constantly to fight the impulse to call Jake herself. After what had happened, the next move was definitely up to him.

She sat near the telephone for the whole weekend, jumping every time it rang, plunged into the depths of despair when it turned out to be Kate or one of her other friends, and pacing around the apartment until she literally had to force herself to get back to work.

Finally, by Sunday night, she was so distraught that she broke her promise to herself and dialled his number. After ten rings, she hung up. He wasn't home. Where was he? Thoughts of blondes flickered through her mind. Would he do that? With a sinking heart, she was afraid the answer was yes.

CHAPTER EIGHT

BY WEDNESDAY Claire was so terrified Jake would never call her again that when he finally did, that very afternoon, and she heard his voice on the other end of the line, she was almost speechless with sheer relief. He, on the other hand, seemed perfectly at ease, and acted as though nothing out of the way had ever happened.

He told her about his busy week, his preparations for a post-season game, the annual recruitment for new players, and ended with a brief apology for not calling sooner.

'How about dinner this weekend?' he asked when he had finished.

By then her heart had settled down to a normal rhythm, and she hesitated for a second before answering. Wasn't he being a little casual about the whole thing, considering she'd gone five whole days without even hearing the sound of his voice? It had been a misery for her, but she *had* survived, after all. Maybe she shouldn't make things quite so easy for him.

'Claire?' she heard him say. 'Are you still there?

'Yes,' she replied. 'I was just thinking. I'm going up to Camano Island to visit my father this weekend.'

'Well, let's make it tonight, then.' His voice lowered.

'I've missed you, Claire. I'd really like to see you.'

Her heart turned over at the low, intimate tone, and she knew she was lost. 'All right,' she agreed. 'Yes, I'd like that.'

They went to the small Greek restaurant near the campus. When he showed up that night at her door, all Claire's misgivings flew out of the window. He looked wonderful, tall and confident, filling her small apartment with his dynamic presence. He was dressed casually in dark trousers, white turtle-neck sweater and a tweed jacket. His dark chestnut-coloured hair gleamed, his eyes were bright, and her only thought was how lucky she was to attract such a man.

The minute she'd let him in, he'd scooped her up in his arms and held her tightly for several long seconds, his face in his hair, his hands stroking slowly up and down her back. When he kissed her, softly, gently, but with passion barely held in check, all her bones turned to jelly, and she was helpless against the powerful attraction he held for her.

At the restaurant, they were seated in the dining-room at a table near the bar, screened from the noisy cocktail lounge by a row of potted palms. A piano was playing show tunes and, as she looked across the table at the man she loved, Claire knew that no matter what happened, no matter what risk she might be taking, just being with him like this made it all worthwhile.

After they'd ordered their drinks, he reached for her hand across the table and held it in his. 'Tell me about your week,' he said. 'Have you been as busy as I have?'

'Oh, it's always busy getting ready for a new term.' She gave him a teasing smile. 'And there'll soon be a whole new crop of athletes doing their darnedest to keep from learning anything worthwhile.'

'Well, at least you won't have me to contend with until next football season. They can do what they please until then. What else has been going on? Any hot gossip in the English department?'

'Let's see. The Dean will be retiring next year, and Curtis is still bucking for the job. It's a plummy spot if he can get it.'

Jake made a face, dismissing Curtis as not worth discussing. Their drinks arrived just then, and Jake released her hand and started fumbling in all his pockets.

'I'm out of cigarettes,' he said, rising from the table. 'There's a machine in the foyer. I'll only be a minute.' As he passed her chair, he put a possessive hand on her shoulder and gave it a little squeeze.

She watched him as he strode away from her, threading his way gracefully around the tables, stopping once or twice to speak briefly to other diners. He seemed to know everybody, and they all seemed eager to claim an acquaintance with him. The man of the hour, Kate had called him, and it was true.

When he was out of sight, Claire leaned her elbows on the table, dreamily sipping her drink, listening to the piano music and the low hum of voices coming from the cocktail-lounge next door, and congratulating herself again on her good fortune. When the music stopped, the voices became louder, a group of men obviously involved in a low, heated discussion, punctuated by bursts of laughter.

They must have been sitting just on the other side of the row of palm trees, because she could hear them quite clearly. However, it wasn't until her own name was mentioned that she paid attention to what they were saying. Then her ears perked up.

'You know who Claire Talbot is,' one of them said. 'That tall, good-looking redhead in the English department. Curtis Gregg's little protégée.'

'Oh, sure,' said another. 'I know who you mean. I never would have thought she was Donovan's type. Not flashy enough.'

There was general laughter, then someone else said, 'Hey, you should know by now that every woman is Jake Donovan's type.'

More laughter, then the first man spoke again. 'She seems like a real iceberg to me, you know, unapproachable. You really think he's scored with her?'

'Well, if he hasn't yet, I'll be glad to give you odds he will in the future. That game plan of his is infallible.'

'Is he still playing around with that blonde? Shirley, I think her name is.'

'Sure he is. I just saw them together last Saturday night. You know Jake. He's too smart to give up a sure thing for a long shot like the Talbot gal.'

As each ugly, hurtful word sank into Claire's numbed brain, the room began to spin. She turned hot, and then cold, then hot again. She'd never felt such shame, such humiliation, such blind rage. It was so degrading! To be discussed like that in the same breath with that Shirley person, who apparently made a career of picking up men in bars!

The piano had started playing again, drowning them out, and she leaned back in her chair, her eyes closed tight. Her stomach was churning, her heart hammering, and her head whirling around crazily.

Then, from what seemed like an enormous distance away, she heard his voice. 'Claire? Are you all right?'

She opened her eyes and looked up to see Jake standing beside her chair, staring down at her with obvious concern. 'No,' she said, rising shakily to her feet. 'I'm not all right. I don't feel well. I think you'd better take me home.'

He took one look at her, then threw some money on the table to pay for their drinks, took her firmly by the arm and guided her out of the restaurant. She could barely stand to have him touch her now, but she gritted her teeth and marched on. She wasn't so sure she could have made it under her own steam anyway, and she wanted badly to get home as soon as possible.

He drove to her place quickly and silently, only darting an occasional worried glance her way. Like most men, she thought scornfully, he was uncomfortable with illness, and she was grateful for the respite from his attentions. The one thing she was determined on was that this was not going to be a repetition of the fiasco at the cabin. There would be no childish sulks this time, and no chance for his clever explanations. It was going to be an open break, and she was going to tell him why.

At her apartment, he started to get out of the car, but before he could open the door, she called to him.

'Jake, don't go. I want to talk to you.'

He turned around, his eyes wide with surprise. 'Sure,' he said. 'I just thought you might want . . .'

'I have something to say to you, Jake, and I want to say it now.' She took a deep breath. 'I don't want to see you any more.'

His eyes narrowed at her and he didn't speak for several seconds. 'Listen, Claire,' he said, 'if this is more of your suspicions about what happened last weekend . . .'

'No,' she broke in. 'It's not.' She felt very calm now that she had made her decision, and went on in a cold, clipped voice. 'I overheard an interesting conversation in the bar tonight while you were out getting cigarettes. Apparently some of your friends were making bets on how long it would take you to get me into bed. I'm surprised at you, Jake. I thought surely you would have announced it to the whole world by now that your game plan had already worked. Well, you can just find yourself another victim. Like Shirley, for instance. But I don't want to play by your rules any more.'

Throughout the long speech, he had several times tried to interrupt, and now she had finally wound down, he finally had his chance. 'Now listen,' he said, 'let me get this straight. You heard some of my friends discussing you tonight. Right?' When she didn't answer, he went on, 'And now you're holding me responsible for what they said. Don't you think that's a little unfair?'

She turned on him with fire in her eyes. 'No!' she cried. 'I don't. It doesn't even matter whether what they said was true or not, not about me and not about the fact that you've been seeing Shirely all along without telling me.'

'I *haven't* been seeing Shirley!' he shouted.

'What about last Saturday night?'

He opened his mouth, then shut it and ran a hand over the back of his neck. 'All right. I guess I forgot. It wasn't important. I'd gone out for dinner alone and ran into her at a place downtown. We had one drink together, and that was it. She's an old friend, for God's sake.'

She didn't believe him. She'd never believe him again. 'It doesn't matter,' she said dully. 'I don't even care. What I do care about is having my name bandied about in bars by drunken playboys. I won't have that, and if seeing you means that's going to happen, then I don't want to see you any more.'

'Claire,' he said softly, 'don't go. I don't want to it end this way. I don't want it to end at all.'

He put a tentative hand on her arm. She looked at him, and when she met his gaze she faltered for a moment. What she saw in the darkened green eyes looked so vulnerable, so pleading, that it could almost have been real love she saw shining there.

Then, as though realising he'd said more than he intended by that look, his face closed in and he withdrew his hand. 'All right,' he said in a low, expressionless tone. 'If that's what you want, I won't argue with you.'

She opened the door and stepped out on to the kerb. Slamming the door shut, she marched off towards her building without a backward glance, propelled inexorably forward by the cold fury that still boiled up within her.

For the next two days, Claire threw herself into her work, every kind of work with with a vengeance. Anything to keep herself from thinking. She planned her class discussions for the next two months; she spent long hours in the library finishing the research for her thesis; she scrubbed every inch of her apartment, washed and ironed all her clothes, and, when all else failed, took long drives by herself. She even debated getting a cat.

On Thursday night she had dinner with her friends as usual. They were all so intent on telling each other about their Christmas activities that Claire was able to keep quiet about her own affairs. Only Kate seemed interested.

'Well,' she said in a low voice while the others talked among themselves, 'how was the trip with Jake? Have you succumbed yet to his manly charms?'

Claire jumped at the mention of his name, the name she'd been struggling so hard to forget, but covered it as best she could. 'It was all right,' she said with a smile.

'Don't fall all over yourself with enthusiasm,' Kate remarked sarcastically. 'Just all right?'

Claire shrugged. 'Oh, you know. I think you were right all along,' she added, knowing it would please Kate. 'He's a little too rich for my blood.'

'Made a serious pass, I take it.'

'Something like that. Anyway, you'll be glad to hear I've decided not to see him any more.'

Kate nodded owlishly. 'A wise move, I think.'

On Saturday she set out early on the drive to Camano Island. She knew the weekend would be the hardest to get through, and she was anxious to visit her father. She hadn't seen Jake since Wednesday night, nor had he called her, and she was grateful for that. If she could just keep him out of her sight and mind, she might be able to forget him eventually.

Her father's house was on the beach, a small cottage he'd bought when he retired from teaching two years ago. Her mother had died several years before that, and he had rattled around in their old family home in the city for far too long as it was. This place just suited him.

Although he seemed glad to see her, she could tell as soon as she got out of her car that he was disappointed she hadn't brought Jake. She didn't say anything about it then, but as soon as she was settled in the spare bedroom, and they were having lunch, she told him about their break-up, as much as she thought he needed to know, at any rate.

When she was through, her father rubbed his chin thoughtfully. He was a mild-mannered man in his early sixties, balding a little and growing a slight paunch, but still handsome.

'Well, I'm sorry to hear that, honey. Of course I don't know him, but from all I've heard about him and the volunteer work he does with young people, he sounds like a fine man.' That was all he said about it, and from then on the subject was closed.

It rained the entire weekend Claire was there, so

that she couldn't even take the long walks alone on the beach she had counted on. Instead, she and her father were cooped up in the small cottage together the entire time, playing cards or watching television, trying to make small talk. The strain of not being able to discuss the one subject paramount in her mind soon began to drive her wild, until finally, by Sunday morning, she was ready to scream.

After breakfast, as they were finishing their second cups of coffee, she told him she wanted to leave that morning. 'I still have a lot to catch up on,' she explained feebly. 'The thesis is all researched now and ready to draft, and my classwork . . .'

'Honey, what's wrong?' he broke in mildly.

She gave him a sharp look over the rim of her cup. 'Nothing's wrong, Dad. I told you. I have a lot to do.'

He sighed deeply and reached across the table to cover her hand with his. 'Claire, no one knows you as I do. You haven't changed much since you were a little bit of a thing. You're just like your mother. You keep too much to yourself. Now, come on, honey. Tell your old Dad what's on your mind. You've been prowling around like a caged lion ever since you got here.'

So she told him. Fighting back the tears, she told him the whole story, even including the night in the cabin, the argument on the way home. But when it came to the conversation she'd overheard in the bar of the Greek restaurant, she merely sketched it in. She hated even thinking about those hurtful words, much less relating them to her own father.

'Well,' he said when she had finished, 'I can see

your point. The man does seem as though he might travel in too fast a lane for a girl like you. Still, reading between the lines of what you *didn't* say, it sounds to me as though you still care about him. Maybe he's worth making a few concessions for.'

'Oh, you men!' she cried irritably, her nerves still raw. 'You always stick together. Well, let me tell you a little bit about the real Jake Donovan.' She went on to describe that awful conversation in more explicit detail, finishing up with, 'Now, is that really the way you like to hear your daughter's name bandied about in bars?'

'No, of course not,' he said with a smile. 'But what did he have to say when you confronted him with it?'

'Oh, the usual. Just something feeble about how it wasn't his fault what his friends say.'

'Well, you'll have to admit, honey, the man has a point.'

'Oh, Dad, don't you see? Even if that's true, and he's as pure as the driven snow, *any* woman Jake Donovan gets involved with will be the target of smutty talk like that. I don't want any part of it.'

'What about the blonde? That sounds a lot more serious then the idle chatter of few drunks. What did he say about her?'

She shrugged. 'Oh, just that he'd run into her by accident and they only had a drink together.'

'Is it entirely out of the question that he's telling the truth?' he asked mildly.

She set her jaw and glared at him. 'You don't understand. You can't possibley know how—how—*dirty* it made me feel when I heard those men talking about me. Or how betrayed I felt after what had happened between us at the thought of him with that woman. I know you mean well, Dad, but you've got to trust my judgement on this. I'm not going to see him again, and that's the end of it.'

She drove the thirty miles back to Seattle in a sleety drizzle. It was going to be a severe winter, according to the experts, and that could mean weeks of ice and snow, a prospect that lowered her depressed spirits even further.

Her apartment seemed particularly cold and barren and damp after the cosy warmth of her father's house. Her first impulse after she'd turned on the heat was to call him and apologise for her childish behaviour. She simply couldn't go on alienating the people she loved most over one bad experience.

The weeks passed slowly and with difficulty, but they did pass, and by the end of January Claire was feeling as though she just might live. Gradually, the whole affair with Jake began to recede in her mind. Her work was going well, her thesis was half drafted, and if Curtis was indeed appointed to fill the Dean's shoes she had a good chance at one of the coveted tenured positions.

Occasionally she would catch a glimpse of Jake at a distance, walking along through the campus or talking to a group of students, and each time she did her heart would flip over, her stomach drop in a sickening thud, her throat choke up. Even that got better after a while, and, since the times she did see him were rare, she finally became convinced that she was really over him.

In early February, she was laid up for a few days with a mild bout of 'flu. Although she didn't have a raging fever, she felt ill enough to miss both her classes and her regular Thursday night dinner with her friends.

The next afternoon, Kate showed up at her apartment with a jar of home-made chicken soup and a stern lecture on taking care of herself.

'Why aren't you in bed?' she demanded severely when Claire answered the door fully dressed.

Claire laughed. 'Because I'm not that sick.'

Kate put a hand on her forehead. 'Well, you don't seem to have a fever,' she admitted grudgingly.

'See? I told you. I'll just rest over the weekend, and by Monday I'll be fine. I haven't felt really awful at all, as a matter of fact. It must be a strange bug. I'm just so queasy in the morning when I get up.' She started to carry the soup into the kitchen. 'How about a cup of coffee?' she called over her shoulder.

She had just put the soup into the fridge when she turned to see that Kate had followed her into the kitchen. She was standing in the doorway staring down at her and frowning thoughtfully.

'Well?' Claire said, straightening up. 'Do you want that coffee or not?'

Kate came walking slowly towards her, eyeing her carefully up and down. 'Have you put on a little weight lately?' she asked.

'Well, maybe a little,' she admitted guiltily.

'And you say you're only sick in the morning?'

'Yes. It's the oddest . . .' She stopped short when

she saw the expression on her friend's face. 'Kate, what wrong?'

'Claire, is it possible you might be pregnant?'

Suddenly the light dawned. As the awful realisation hit her she began to put two and two together, remembering some other odd symptoms that had puzzled her in the last few weeks. How could she possibly have missed it? The one night she'd spent with Jake had been so successfully blotted out of her memory that such a possibility had never entered her head.

She gave Kate one horrified look, then with a loud groan she staggered blindly to a chair, sank down slowly, and buried her face in her hands.

'Now, listen,' Kate said sternly. She sat down beside Claire and put an arm around her heaving shoulders. 'Don't panic. The first thing to do is see a doctor and make sure.' She paused for a moment, then went on in a softer tone, 'I take it, then, that there is a possibility?'

Claire raised her head and gazed bleakly at her friend. Her whole world was falling apart. She couldn't choke out a word to save her life. All she could do was nod, then she burst into tears.

When the doctor confirmed her worst fears a few days later, Claire was numb with dazed unbelief and beside herself with panic, hardly able to take in this terrible thing that had happened to her. Then, after a day or two, as she calmed down, she realised she had to make some plans.

The first thing, of course was to decide whether she could go through with it. Abortion was legal now, and there would be no problem there. But she dismissed that alternative instantly. To her, the life she was carrying was already a human being, with a whole heredity programmed into its genes and chromosomes from the moment of conception.

Well, what then? Adoption? She couldn't bear the thought of giving her child away for someone else to raise. She'd just have to do it alone. Other women did it nowadays. It wasn't the stigma it used to be. She could think of at least two other instructors at the college who were single mothers. It could be worked out.

The doctor prescribed medication for her morning sickness, so at least she was able to keep on with her teaching. No one would find out about it for several months. And by then maybe she'd be more used to the idea herself.

Kate was wonderful, spending long hours with her, discussing the problem endlessly, making sure she ate, listening to her cry. They came close to an argument just once, a week after Claire's visit to the doctor.

They were in Claire's kitchen drinking coffee early one evening, and had just had gone through the whole gumut of alternatives for what seemed like the hundredth time—abortion, adoption, keeping the baby—when out of a clear blue sky, Kate said, 'You know, Claire, I really think you should tell Jake.'

Claire turned and gazed at her in horror. 'Never!' she cried. 'I absolutely don't won't him to find out.'

'Well, I don't see why not. Damn it, it's his responsibility, too. Besides, he has a right to know.'

'He has no rights whatsoever,' Claire said firmly.

'Or any responsibility, either, for that matter. I knew what I was doing, and I knew what kind of man he was. Besides, what could he do?'

Kate shrugged helplessly. 'I don't know. Maybe help with the money? Maybe even marry you. He may be a playboy, but he doesn't strike me as a totally irresponsible man, and I'll bet he'd want to do the honourable thing.'

'Oh, come on, Kate. The man is paranoid about marriage, if that's what you mean by the "honourable thing". That's not what I want, anyway. I'd rather raise my child alone than force any man into a loveless marriage.'

'But he must have cared something about you, or this never would have happened in the first place,' Kate argued reasonably.

Claire gave a bitter laugh. 'Oh, he cared, all right. It flattered his ego to make a conquest of what his friends call the "iceberg schoolteacher", to add another *floozy* to his list so he could joke about it with is friends.'

Kate goggled at her. 'Floozy?' She shook her head slowly. 'Honestly, Claire, I don't know where you come up with these archaic terms. Probably out of some book.'

'You know very well what I mean.'

'And just how many "floozies" has he taken home to meet his family?' Kate demanded. 'Doesn't that mean anything?'

Suddenly, the conversation she'd had with Jake's sister flashed into Claire's mind. Linda had made a point of telling her that Jake had never brought another woman to her house. Then another image quickly followed, the strange, haunted look on his face the night of their final break.

There had been something in his eyes then, a fleeting hint of terrible vulnerability, even pain, as though he cared more about her than he was willing to admit and was truly sorry to lose her.

But that way lay madness, and she dismissed it instantly. He may have been hurt that night, but only because one of his amorous adventures had backfired on him. And in the very next moment, when he agreed with her that it was best to part, the look of relief on his face was unmistakable.

'No,' she said to Kate, 'it doesn't mean a thing. The man is incapable of honest emotion, and I don't want to hear any more about it. I'll manage this by myself.' She gave Kate a stern look of warning. 'I don't want Jake to know, Kate.'

'But he'll have to find out about it some time, Claire.'

Claire got up from the table and carried their cups over to the kitchen sink. 'I know that, but don't forget the old saying,' she called lightly over her shoulder. 'Only the woman knows for sure. Let him think what he likes, but I'm not telling him, and I don't want you to, either.'

It turned out to be an exceptionally cold February, so cold that the intermittent snowfalls remained on the ground, frozen solid, even during the clear, sunny spells in between.

The winter days were still quite short, and Claire

found that to be a blessing. Although her morning sickness was gone at last, she was so constantly tired these days that she was glad to fall exhausted into bed well before ten o'clock at night.

One Thursday night in late February, she had just settled down at her desk to correct the day's test papers when a knock came at her door. She raised her head and frowned, wondering who could be dropping by at this hour. It was past nine-thirty, and after a late supper she had already changed into her nightclothes. Her hair was gathered into a long plait that hung down her back, her face was scrubbed, and she was in no mood to entertain visitors.

When the knock came again, with more urgency this time, she sighed deeply, took off her glasses and got up from the desk. Tying her robe more tightly around her waist, she went to the door, checked to make sure the chain bolt was secure, and in the next interval between the loud pounding knocks, called out, 'Who's there?'

'It's me,' came Jake's voice. 'Let me in. I've got to talk to you.'

Her heart lurched sickeningly, and she clutched tightly at the opening of her robe. 'No!' she cried. He was the *last* person on earth she wanted to see right now.

'Come on, Claire,' he said in a low earnest tone. 'I won't stay long. I just want to talk.'

'I don't want to talk to you, Jake. We have nothing to say to each other. Now, will you please go away?'

She was standing close to the door, her ear pressed against it. There was a dead silence on the other side. She held her breath, hoping he had left, listening for his footsteps. Then he spoke again.

'If you don't let me in by the count of three, I'm going to bash this door down.' There was a slight pause. 'One,' he said in an ominous tone.

He meant it. He was perfectly capable, both physically and mentally, of breaking in bodily. Her mind raced. What would the neighbours say? Would someone call the police? Should *she* call the police?

'Two,' came the firm voice.

'Oh, all right,' she said.

She slipped the chain-bolt, turned the latch, and opened the door. He stood there for a moment looking down at her, grim-faced and haggard. He was wearing shabby blue jeans and a heavy sheepskin jacket with the collar turned up at the back of his neck.

Without a word, he brushed past her and strode purposefully to the middle of the living-room. He stood there, facing away from her, his broad shoulders hunched over his hands shoved in his jacket pocket, staring down at the floor. Claire shut the door and walked over to him.

'You've got five minutes,' she said, 'and then I'm calling the police.'

He spun around to face her, his features taut and strained, his expression livid. 'I just discovered your little secret,' he ground out at last.

She looked away from him, biting her lip. Oh, God, she thought. It was the last thing she wanted. Still, he would have to know sooner or later. She turned back to face him. He was still glowering down at her, waiting.

'All right,' she said with a shrug. 'So now you know. How did you find out?' It had to be Kate.

He waved a hand dismissively in the air. 'That doesn't matter. What I came here to find out is why the hell you didn't tell me about it yourself.'

'Why should I?'

He winced visibly at that, and quickly turned his head away, but there was no mistaking the momentary spasm of pain that had crossed his fine features. Claire felt a sudden wave of sympathy for him, but then checked it immediately. He had no right whatsoever to come barging in here like this, demanding answers to his questions.

When he looked at her again, his gaze had softened. He took a step towards her, one hand tentatively held out before him. 'Don't you think I have a right to know that you're carrying my child?'

She raised her chin and gazed directly into his glittering green eyes. 'What makes you so sure it's your child?'

His mouth dropped open, and he jerked his head back as though warding off a physical blow.

'Are you telling me it's not?' he asked quietly. 'Because if you are, you're a liar. I may be dense about a lot of things. Claire, but one thing I would stake my life on is that I was the only man in your life at the time you must have conceived that child.'

She had no answer to that. She couldn't lie to him, and she was already ashamed of her hurtful words. Even though he might have betrayed her trust and made her a laughing-stock among his friends, the man did have feelings. He did suffer. And he wasn't an evil or vindictive person.

'All right,' she said with a sigh. 'But it doesn't make any difference. It's still my problem, my responsibility. I don't expect you to . . .'

He reached out and grabbed her firmly by the arms. 'It's my responsiblility, too, Claire,' he said, looking down deeply into her eyes. 'And I intend to fulfil it.'

'There's really nothing you can do, Jake,' she said wearily. 'The college has excellent medical coverage. I suppose later on if you wanted to contribute something to its support . . .'

'I'm not talking about money,' he said harshly. His fingers bit into her arms.

'Well, what then?'

'There's only one answer. I want to marry you.'

CHAPTER NINE

'YOU want to what?'

'You heard me. I think we should get married.'

If he hadn't been holding her arms so tightly, she would have slid to he floor. It was the last thing she'd expected. Marry him? For one brief moment, her heart soared. Then she came down to earth with a dull thud.

'You can't be serious,' she said.

'I'm dead serious.'

She gave him a twisted smile. 'Well, thanks for the offer, Jake. It's very generous of you. But it's out of the question.'

'Why?' he shot back at her.

'Why? Well there are a hundred reasons.'

'Name one.'

'What's the point? It's just not possible.'

'Listen,' he said, releasing her, 'could we sit down? Maybe have some of that brandy of yours?' He led her over to the couch. 'Here, you sit down. I'll get the brandy.'

When he had disappeared into the kitchen, she laid her head back, closed her eyes and tried to think. But the noise he made rattling around in her cupboards distracted her, and by the time he came back she was still in a daze.

He only had one glass with him, and he held it up.

'I don't think you should drink spirits in your condition,' he said soberly. 'Can't I make you a cup of tea? Get you a glass of milk?'

'No, thanks,' she replied weakly.

He sat down beside her, settled back comfortably and took a long swallow of brandy. Then he set the glass on the coffee-table and turned to her, his arm stretched along the back of the couch.

'Now, here's what I think we should do,' he began. 'I have to go out of town first thing in the morning. There's an important meeting with the pro football association in Dallas about getting the Super Bowl held in Seattle next year. But I'll only be gone two days at the most, and as soon as I get back we'll get a licence and get married. A few more days won't make any difference, and . . .'

'Jake!' she broke in. 'Will you please stop that?'

He looked over at her in surprise. 'Well, I admit I'm moving a little fast, but the timing is pretty important here. We don't want to saddle the kid with a stigma before he's born, do we?'

'Jake, I've been trying to tell you. I can't marry you.'

'Now, that's nonsense. I may not be the world's prize catch, or anyone's notion of ideal husband material, but I'd do my best. And I think I'd make a hell of a father.'

'Listen, Jake, before you get too carried away, will you please answer one question?'

He nodded. 'Sure. What is it?'

'Just this. If there had been no baby, would you still have wanted to marry me?'

He frowned and looked away. Without a word, he picked up his glass and took another swallow of brandy. Then he reached in his pocket for his cigarettes, lit one, and dropped the spent match in the ashtray on the table. Finally, he turned back to her.

'I can't answer that question, Claire,' he said gravely. 'Marriage was never part of my plans for my life. I never made any secret about that, it was clear from the very first.'

'Then what would this marriage mean to you?'

'Well,' he said with a shrug, 'I guess the important thing is to give our child a stable home.'

She had to ask. Gathering up all her courage, she said softly, 'And what about me, Jake? How do you feel about me?'

She could literally see him squirming as he shifted his position and leaned forward to grind out his half-smoked cigarette. 'You shouldn't have to ask that,' he said at last. 'I was crazy about you when we were together, you know that.'

She closed her eyes again, trying to think. He didn't love her, that much was clear, and she didn't dare press it any further. In a way he was right. Perhaps the only important issue here was the welfare of the child she was carrying. In Jake's mind he was doing the honourable thing, making an enormous concession for the sake of another human being, even to the extent of giving up his precious freedom.

But for how long? And would she be able to tolerate it when he began to stray into another woman's bed?

'How about it, Claire?' he was saying. 'Will you do it? Will you marry me?'

She opened her eyes and looked at him. 'All right, Jake. I'll marry you.' She had to think of the child first, and this was the only possible choice she could make. Heaven help her if it turned out to be the worst one.

'Good,' he said with satisfaction. 'You won't be sorry.' He glanced at his watch and rose to his feet. 'I'd better go now. I still have to pack for my trip, and my plane leaves at six o'clock in the morning.'

He picked up his brandy, lifted his head to drain the last of it, then set his glass down on the table. Before leaving, he leaned over to kiss her lightly on the forehead. 'It'll be all right, Claire,' he said softly. 'You'll see.' He straightened up and moved swiftly to the door, where he stood for a moment looking back at her.

'I'll call you as soon as I get back. Should be Sunday, Monday at the latest. Then we'll see about that licence. In the meantime, think happy thoughts.'

When he was gone, the room seemed suddenly cold and empty, and Claire continued to sit motionless on the couch where he had left her, still in a daze. His calm confidence had reassured her somewhat, but now the doubts began to return. Finally, with a heavy sigh, she got up and carried his glass and the ashtray he had used into the kitchen.

At least Dad will be thrilled, she thought, as she rinsed them at the sink. To have Jake Donovan for a son-in-law would be considered quite a coup among his cronies. And he would be a good father, he was right about that. But what kind of husband he would make hardly bore thinking about.

* * *

The next afternoon right after lunch, Claire drove up to Camano Island to see her father. She wanted to tell him the news in person, and hadn't even called him to let him know she was coming.

Ever since Jake had left last night, her spirits had gradually lifted to the point where now, as she drove north on the interstate past the frozen landscape, still white with the accumulated snow of the past month, she actually felt happy, for the first time in weeks.

It wasn't just the fact that all her practical problems would be solved by his unexpected proposal of marriage, although that was an enormous relief. Raising a child alone had been a far more frightening prospect than she had admitted, even to herself. But more—much more—she would actually be the wife of the man she loved, had never stopped loving.

She'd called Kate that morning to tell her. She owed her that much after the enormous help and support she'd provided through the most difficult part of her adjustment. As she'd expected, Kate was pleased, but full of warnings.

'I only hope you understand exactly what you might be letting yourself in for, Claire,' she'd said carefully. 'I mean, you're such a romantic at heart. I'm just afraid you might be setting your sights too high and expecting more from him than he has any intention of delivering.'

'Don't worry, Kate. I may be a romantic, I think I have my share of common sense as well, and I'm not a complete idiot. Believe me, I'm going into this marriage with my eyes wide open. It's for the child's sake, and that's all.'

She knew, of course, exactly what Kate meant. She was also well aware that she was fudging just a little to Kate. Although it was anybody's guess how long Jake intended to remain faithful, she couldn't help hoping that, if she tried hard, they might be able to build a real marriage. She hadn't raised that aspect of it at all with Jake last night, and she wasn't going to in the future. He didn't love her, not the way she loved him. But she believed he was fond of her, and that would have to be enough.

The freeway was almost deserted today because of the uncertain weather. Although the sun was shining at the moment, more snow was predicted for that evening, and Claire planned to spend the night at her father's in the hope of missing the worst of it.

By now she had gone past the scattered small towns that lay north of the city and was just approaching the tricky interchange, a wide, looping cloverleaf shape, that would take her off the interstate and on to the secondary road that led to the island.

Slowing down cautiously as she turned on to the ramp, she carefully manoeuvred the first broad bend in the road. Then, directly ahead of her, her eyes was caught by a dark glint on the pavement where the pale sunshine caught it, just around the next curve.

But before the meaning of that shiny patch of road could register in her brain, she was on top of the black ice. As she lost traction and started slipping, she fought for control, frantically braking and twisting the steering wheel. The car went into a spin, and the last thing she saw was the white metal guard-rail coming up to meet her. There was an impact, a sickening thud, and then blackness descended.

It seemed as though she was slowly emerging from the dark tunnel towards the daylight. Gradually, as she regained consciousness, her eyes fluttered open. She was lying on a strange bed in an unfamiliar room. Everything was white and there was a pungent antiseptic odour in the warm, close air.

Then she remembered. The ice, the car spinning, the last impact. She'd been in an accident.

But obviously she was alive. Gingerly she tested her muscles, arms, legs, shoulders, back. Everything seemed to be in working order. She moved her head tentatively to the right and saw a shape, dim and dark against the bright light. Focusing her eyes on it, the image gradually clarified into a woman standing by the side of the bed.

She was dressed in white, obviously a nurse, and she bent over Claire now, her hand on her forehead. 'Well, honey, how are you feeling?'

'Where am I?'

The nurse chuckled. 'Same old question. You're in the hospital at Stanwood. Your car crashed on a patch of ice.'

'How long have I been here?'

'Just overnight. Today is Saturday. You were brought in early yesterday afternoon.'

'How—how badly am I hurt?'

The nurse gave her a cheerful smile and patted her shoulder. 'You're hardly hurt at all. Luckily you had your seat-belt on, and although you were badly shaken up, there's no serious damage. Just a few minor bruises.'

'What does that mean?' She tried to sit up, and the room immediately began to whirl around.

The nurse pushed her shoulders gently back on the bed. 'Take it easy, now. Don't try to sit up or get out of bed. I'll get the doctor. He'll answer all your questions.'

When she was gone, Claire closed her eyes. She wasn't seriously hurt. The nurse had told her that, and she wouldn't lie. Nothing seemed to be broken and her head was beginning to clear. But what about the baby? How badly could one be 'shaken up' and still sustain that life within?

In a few minutes a very young doctor came into her room. 'Well, now, Miss Talbot, how are you feeling?'

'I'm fine, doctor. But please tell me . . .'

'Just a minute,' he broke in. 'Let me check you over first, then I'll answer your questions.'

While he poked and prodded and listened through his stethoscope and tested her reflexes and shone his light into her eyes, Claire tried to control her fears. Both the doctor and the nurse were being a little too evasive.

'Well,' he said at last, beaming, 'no concussion, no internal injuries. Everything looks fine to me.'

'The baby,' she said impatiently. 'What about the baby?'

Immediately he sobered. 'I'm afraid you lost it,' he said, peering down solemnly at her. Then, hastily, he added, 'But if it's any consolation, you probably would have miscarried eventually, anyway. An impact like that would be traumatic in any case, and even if you'd managed to hang on another week or month, there would have been problems ahead for you.'

Then he brightened. 'Luckily, your pregnancy was in its very earliest stages, so that you should suffer no ill effects at all from the miscarriage. And you're young. There's no reason in the world why you shouldn't go on to have healthy babies in the future. So, you see, it's not the end of the world.'

Maybe not to you, she thought bitterly, but it might as well be for me. Fighting back the tears, she looked up at him. 'I want to go home as soon as possible. When can I leave?'

'Not for a day or two. You seem fine now, but I'd like to keep you under observation for at least twenty-four hours.'

Today was Saturday. Jake was due back tomorrow or the day after. She had to be there when he arrived.

Once again she tried to sit up, and this time she managed to prop herself up on her elbows with only a slight dizziness. 'I have to go home today,' she said flatly. 'It's important.'

The doctor gave her a long, appraising look, his chin in his hand. 'It would be better if you stayed another night.'

'Please,' she said, 'I must go home today.'

'Well,' he said dubiously, 'I guess it would be all right so long as someone could pick you up. You shouldn't try to drive for a while. And I want you to promise me that you'll check in with your own doctor in a day or two, just to make sure we didn't miss something.'

* * *

Kate and Harold came that afternoon to get her and take her home. A warm front had moved into the area during the night, turning the promised snow into rain, and although the drive home under grey skies and a steady downpour was gloomy, at least the ice had melted, and it was a quick trip.

Kate wisely remained silent during the entire drive, her inquisitiveness checked not only by her husband's presence, but by the curt way Claire had informed her about what had happened on the telephone. Even she seemed to realise that the subject was closed for now.

At the apartment, Kate helped her inside, insisting all along the way that she get right into bed and offering to stay with her. Claire stubbornly resisted both suggestions.

'I'm perfectly all right, Kate,' she said. 'I appreciate your coming to get me today, I really do. You were a life-saver. I couldn't stand another minute in that hospital. But the doctor assured me there's nothing really wrong, and I believe him. I don't want to go to bed, and I really would like to be alone. OK?'

'Sure. I understand.'

'And thank Harold again for me. I hope I haven't ruined his weekend.'

At the door, before she left, Kate put a hand on Claire's arm. 'I'm sorry about the baby,' she said in a low voice. 'But it might just be for the best.'

The hot tears burned Claire's eyes, and she knew she'd break down if she talked about it now, even to Kate. She meant well, but it was still too soon.

'I know,' she said shakily. 'It'll be all right.'

When Kate finally left and Claire was blessedly

alone in the quiet apartment, she went into the bathroom and ran a hot bath. Every muscle ached, and she still felt a little shaken. While the bath filled, she studied her reflection in the bathroom mirror.

Her hair was a mess, her clothes were rumpled and a seam had split in her jacket. Otherwise, she still looked the same, just a little pale. She didn't know what she had expected to find there. Nothing of the ache in her heart really showed.

She quickly shed her clothes, and as she lowered her aching body into the steaming bath, she allowed the tears to flow freely for the first time since she learned of her loss. It was all over now. All her plans had crumbled to dust. There would be no baby to love now, and no marriage to Jake.

After her bath, she stretched out on top of her bed and immediately fell sound asleep. She woke up some time later to pitch darkness and the sudden realisation that she was famished. She gingerly stretched her sore muscles, then got off the bed, put on a robe, and went into the kitchen to warm up some soup.

For the rest of that Saturday night and all of Sunday morning, she rehearsed the speech she would make to Jake. She wouldn't cry, she promised herself. She didn't want to be an object of pity to anyone at all, but especially not him. She would be calm, even try to be cheerful. It wasn't the end of the world. It just seemed that way.

After a good night's sleep and a light breakfast, she was feeling much stronger. She had dressed that morning in a pair of grey flannel trousers and a striped silk blouse, brushed her hair back and caught it with a clasp so that it hung down her back, and applied a touch of pale lipstick.

When the knock came on her door, early that afternoon, she thought it was probably Kate. Jake had said Sunday or Monday, and that meant Sunday night at the earliest.

When she opened the door to see Jake standing in the hallway, all her carefully rehearsed speeches fled from her mind on the spot. He had on a business suit, his raincoat over his arm, his dark hair damp from the steady drizzle still coming down outside. She could only stand and stare. He looked so wonderful, so *alive*, so *real*.

'I'm back,' he announced with a grin.

'So I see,' she said unsteadily, and opened the door wider.

When he was inside, he threw his coat over a chair, then turned to her and held out his arms. 'Come here,' he said.

She looked away. 'Jake, I have something to say to you.'

He frowned and dropped his arms at his sides. 'Now, don't tell me you've changed your mind about getting married. We went all through that before I left. In fact, I left the meeting a day early, just so we could get going on the licence first thing in the morning. We don't want to delay.' He took a step towards her. 'You know, Claire, while I was away, I had a lot of time to think about this whole thing, and the more I mulled it over, the more excited I got. I liked the idea of being a father, right from the beginning, but there's more to it than that. I want you to know that I have every intention of being a good husband to you, too, Claire, so don't even think of backing out on me now.'

His face was so serious, his whole bearing so sincere, that it was all Claire could do to keep from bursting into tears. He had moved another step closer and stood now looking down at her. A kind of light she'd never seen before was glowing in the green eyes. He looked so happy, so pleased with the way things had turned out, that she yearned to fall into his waiting arms, to feel them around her once again, strong, protecting, a haven of safety.

She could go ahead and marry him now and he'd never know the difference. She wouldn't have to tell him until it was all done. He said he wanted to be a good husband. Maybe that would be enough to hold him.

But she knew she couldn't do that to him. What kind of marriage would they have if it was based on a lie? She wanted him with all her heart, wanted him more than she ever had before, but she had to give him up. *Because* she loved him, she couldn't deceive him.

With every ounce of strength she possessed, she backed away from him, took a deep breath and blurted out, 'Jake, on Friday afternoon, on my way to Camano Island to visit my father, I had an accident in the car. I lost the baby. You don't have to marry me, after all.'

He reared back as though she had struck him in the face. His face darkened with sudden pain. He opened his mouth, but no sound came out. Then he turned from her and walked slowly over to the window. He stood there for a long time, his shoulders bent, his hands in his pockets, staring out at the cold bleak rain.

'I know how you must feel,' she said in a low voice. 'I was disappointed, too.'

He turned around then, and the distance between them, a mere ten feet, seemed more like ten miles. 'Are you all right?' he said at last.

'Oh, yes. I'm fine. Just shaken up a little. The doctor said that it was so early in the pregnancy that I should have no ill effects at all.'

'Well, that's a relief,' he said. 'But I'm damned sorry, Claire, about the baby.' He smiled crookedly at her, and shook his head slowly from side to side. 'I was really looking forward to being a father. Never thought I'd see the day.'

'Well, there's still time for you, Jake,' she said lightly. Then she gave a nervous little laugh and rushed on, 'Of course, now there's no reason to get married.'

'No,' he said. 'I guess not.'

He looked away, as though the subject embarrassed him, and Claire's stomach twisted into a knot of pain. He stood staring down at the floor for several moments, then walked slowly over to the chair where he had thrown his coat and picked it up.

'If you don't need me for anything,' he said, 'I guess I'll be on my way, then. I came here directly from the airport, and I feel like the inside of dustbin. I'd like to go home and clean up.'

'Yes, of course,' she said quickly. 'I understand.'

He raised a hand awkwardly in the air. 'Well, I

guess I'll be seeing you, then.'

With that he was gone, out of her apartment and out of her life. As she stood there, listening to his footsteps fading away down the hall, a cold chill gripped her heart. She felt so alone.

It wasn't ten minutes, however, before he was back. She'd been so depressed by the way he'd left her so abruptly that she hadn't even thought to bolt the door after him, and he simply burst inside.

'Jake!' she said, alarmed. 'What is it?'

He was standing there rigid, his arms crossed over his chest, his long legs apart, glaring down at her. She put a hand to her throat. Did he blame her for losing his child?

'It's just this, Claire.' He hesitated, then in a loud, firm voice of the utmost finality, he blurted out, 'I want to marry you anyway, baby or no baby.'

His lean face was suffused with colour, and there was a strange look of mild astonishment on it, as though he had startled even himself with his unequivocal announcement.

Claire groped weakly behind her for support. Clinging to one arm of the couch, she gradually sank down on to it and stared up at him, certain she had misunderstood what he had just said. Either that or he had not really grasped the fact that there was no child.

'Jake, I don't think you realise what you're saying. I know you've had a shock, that you were counting on being a father, but it's over. Don't you see?'

In one swift movement, he strode over to the couch and sat down beside her. He reached out and took both her hands in his. 'I know exactly what I'm saying,' he said, his eyes boring into hers. 'Now, listen to me. Don't say anything, just listen. I admit it was a blow to me to find out you'd lost the baby, just when I'd decided I really liked the idea. And I admit in the beginning I wasn't exactly thrilled with the thought of giving up my freedom to raise that child with you.'

'I understand that, Jake, and I appreciated . . .'

He put a finger on her mouth, silencing her. 'Wait a minute. I want to say this right.' He frowned, then went on, 'It wasn't until I left here a few minutes ago and started walking out to the car that it suddenly dawned on me. There can always be more children, I thought to myself. But there's only one Claire.'

As his words sank in, Claire's heart soared, but in the next instant her self-protective instincts took over, and she returned to reality with a bang. It was one thing to risk marriage with this man for the sake of an unborn child, but quite another now that that powerful incentive no longer existed.

'Jake,' she said reasonably, 'you don't know what you're saying. You've said it yourself a hundred times. You're not cut out for marrige.'

'I wasn't,' he replied promptly. 'Not until I met you. I enjoyed my life the way it was, I never made any secret of that. But then you came along, and I'd never known a woman quite like you. When you broke off with me that night, it was just as though a light went out of my life, and I began to realise just how empty and meaningless my whole existence had been before you.'

He reached out for her then, but she drew back,

still not convinced he was really serious. There was too much history, too many hurts in the past for her to overcome every hurdle in an instant. She couldn't allow him to push her into a commitment they might both be sorry for. It would be too cruel if she got her hopes up now, only to have him change his mind later.

She rose to her feet and stood looking at him. 'Jake, you're upset. You don't know what you're saying. I think you should leave now. Think it over for a few days, then if you want . . .'

'No!' he said in a loud firm voice. He stood up and took her by the shoulders. 'There's nothing to think about. This isn't a momentary impulse, and it isn't because I'm upset.'

She turned her head away, unable to face him, but as he pressed her closer a familiar warmth began to creep over her. If only she didn't care so much for him! If only he didn't have this power over her!

'Jake, too much has happened in the past to make me believe you'd be willing to settle for one woman. There's a lot of hurt to get over, and a lot of misunderstanding.'

'I think I know what you're talking about. It's still that damned conversation you overheard in the bar that night. Well, just for the record, the next day I made it known in explicit terms that Claire Talbot was off limits as a topic of gossip among that gang of perverts. You won't ever have to worry about that again.'

He held her at arms' length and looked down earnestly into her eyes. 'There's something else I should tell you that might help you understand,' he said slowly. 'Something you probably don't know about me. I was married once, very briefly, right out of college. It didn't last. We were just kids, actually, and neither of us ready for marriage. I was probably largely to blame. I was playing pro football then, and pretty impressed with my own importance. I just didn't realise that she needed more attention than I was willing to give her.'

Claire listened to the history, just as his sister had told it to her, except that in Jake's version he took the blame himself, with no mention of the fact that it was his wife who had betrayed him with other men.

'Anyway,' he went on, 'not only did that experience leave me utterly disillusioned about marriage, but right about then my career really took off, and I found it a very ego-satisfying sensation to be pursued by all the young football groupies who literally follow teams around the country, offering themselves on a plate to the players. Even when I quit pro ball a few years back, there was still plenty of opportunity. I'm not proud of the fact that I took advantage of it, but I got sick of it after a while.' He shrugged. 'I'm not claiming I lived like a monk after that, but I did become much more selective. The trouble was, by then I had built up a reputation for myself that was hard to live down, and my friends just expected things of me that didn't really interest me that much any more.'

'And what about Shirley?'

'I was telling you the absolute truth about that. Shirely is an old friend, and that's all. She has her own reputation to live down, and we do each other favours occasionally. And if you'll recall, that night she and I left the bar together, I was back by the time you were attacked out in the car park.'

She'd been so frightened that night that she'd forgotten he'd only been with Shirely less than half an hour before it happened. And he was right about another thing. She had automatically *expected* the worst of him, just because of his reputation.

For the first time, she began to believe he really meant it when he said he still wanted to marry her. Did she dare to hope? She was having trouble thinking at all with his hands moving on her back, his face so close to hers, the strong, clean, masculine scent of him, the hard body pressing against her.

He cupped her face in his hands. 'I know you don't have much reason to trust me, and I realise I've hurt you in the past, but most of it was sheer misunderstanding, and I swear to you I've never lied to you or deceived you. Except,' he added with a sheepish grin. 'for one thing.'

Claire steeled herself. 'And what's that?'

He folded her closer to him and put his mouth to her ear. 'Just that I love you,' he whispered. Then he drew his head back and looked down into her eyes. 'That's the first time I've ever said that to a woman,' he said with a slow smile. 'And darned if it wasn't nearly as hard as I thought it would be.' He bent to kiss her briefly on the mouth. 'I love you,' he said aloud. 'Darling Claire, my wonderful Claire, I love you.' Then he sobered. 'Can I at least hope that you might be able to love me a little? That you can try to forget the misunderstandings of the past? I swear to you that you can trust me to be faithful to you forever. I know what I want now, and it's worth everything to me.'

'Oh, Jake, I've always loved you,' she cried at last. She threw her arms around his neck and held him tightly to her.

His mouth came down on hers then in a tender kiss, his lips moving softly on her mouth. As the tension built between them, she tossed aside her last inhibition and allowed her hands to run freely, up into his dark, crisp hair, down over his broad shoulders, to rest against his hard, muscular chest, where she could feel the pounding of his heart.

He led her over to the couch and pulled her down beside him. When he reached out for her, she sank happily into his arms.

'Jake, there's one thing I don't understand,' she said. 'If you really cared for me, why did you agree so readily when I told you I didn't want to see you again? You seemed so relieved that I assumed it was what you wanted, too.'

He raised his eyebrows. 'I was terrified of you, that's why.'

'Terrified?' she exclaimed. 'Of me?'

He nodded grimly. 'I knew by then you'd got under my skin and that I was in real danger of falling in love with you. At the time, I not only didn't want to give up my precious freedom, but even more frightening to me was the risk of having a marriage go sour again.' He smiled crookedly. 'And knowing you, I also knew it had to be marriage or nothing. Be honest, now, you know darned well you would never have been happy with an affair.'

'No,' she said slowly, 'you're probably right. I thought so at the time, but I don't know how long I could have tolerated it.'

'Well,' he said with a shrug, 'I felt the same way. You're a serious person, Claire, a genuine person, someone I could see being faithful to the rest of my life. I just didn't really feel I could risk that, and when you called it off I decided—stupidly, I see now—to go along with it.'

He kissed her deeply then, and as his hands began to move urgently over the curves of her body, a wayward thought popped into her mind. Jake Donovan's famous game plan! It had backfired on him at last. In spite of herself, she couldn't resist a little chuckle against his mouth.

He raised his head. 'What's so funny?'

'Nothing, darling,' she said, throwing her arms around his neck and forcing his head back down. 'Nothing at all.'